GETTYSBURG
Crisis of Command

GETTYSBURG
Crisis of Command

Harry Albright

HIPPOCRENE BOOKS
New York

Acknowledgments

Of the many sources consulted in the writing of this study of command in crisis, the following distinguished volumes have been of the greatest value: *R. E. Lee* by Douglas Southall Freeman. Charles Scribner's Sons, New York/London 1934; *Lee's Lieutenants* by Douglas Southall Freeman. Charles Scribner's Sons, New York/London 1943; *The Blue and the Gray* by Henry Steele Commager. The Bobbs-Merrill Company, Inc., New York/1950; *Battles and Leaders of the Civil War* edited by Ned Bradford. Appleton-Century-Crofts, Inc., New York/ 1956; *The Battle of Gettysburg* by Frank Aretas Haskell, edited by Bruce Catton. Houghton Mifflin Co., Boston/1958.

I would like to thank the following libraries for the help they provided me in the gathering of information for this book: Tripler Army Hospital, Fort Shafter Army Library and the Aina Haina Public Library in Honolulu.

For information, contact
Hippocrene Books, Inc.
171 Madison Avenue
New York, NY 10016

Library of Congress Cataloging-in-Publication Data

Albright, Harry.
  Gettysburg : crisis of command / Harry Albright.
  ISBN 0-87052-787-8
   1. Gettysburg, Battle of, 1863—Fiction. 2. United States-
-History—Civil War, 1861–1865—Fiction. I. Title.
  PS3551.L285G4   1989
  813'.54—dc20   89-35151
                                                                CIP

Printed in the United States.

*To Marcia, Carolyn
and Roger*

Contents

Part III *Select your ground and make the enemy attack you.*
                                        —Napoleon

Part IV *The die is cast.*
                                        —Plutarch

Part V *All delays are dangerous in war.*
                                        —John Dryden

Part VI *You can ask me for anything you like, except time.*
                                        —Napoleon

Part I

To Confuse and Confound.
        —Robert E. Lee to Thomas
Jonathan Jackson, November 14,
                                1862

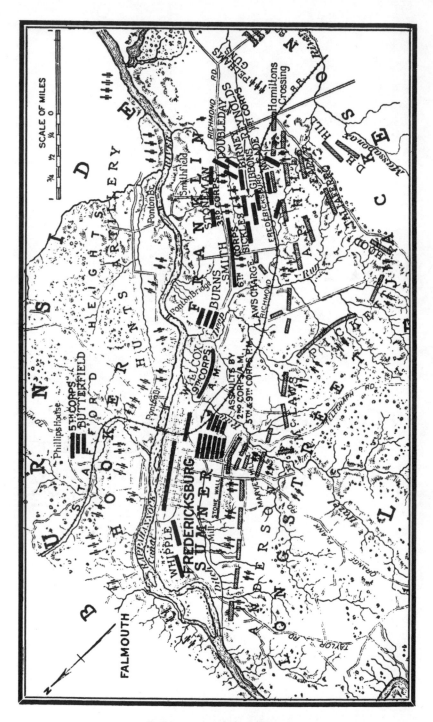

Battle of Fredericksburg.

1

Farewell to Little Mac

TWO HORSEMEN DISMOUNTED IN A SWIRLING SNOWSTORM that late November night before the headquarters tent of the commanding general of the Army of Northern Virginia of the Confederate States of America. It was still the bloody year of 1862, reeling from the shock of the killing at the little town of Sharpsburg on the banks of Antietam Creek only two months before.

While they were handing over their reins to a soldier, the commanding general himself, Robert E. Lee, came out to greet them in the cold, for the pair were the newly promoted Lieutenant General Thomas Jonathan Jackson and his aide, Captain J. P. Smith. Their arrival had been eagerly awaited by Lee, for he had summoned "Stonewall" to lead his Second Corps eastward out of the Shenandoah

Valley to rejoin the main army at the old colonial town of Fredericksburg.

In his warning orders he had written Jackson: "We will endeavor to confuse and confound the enemy as much as our circumstances will permit."

To this end the conversation after supper turned to the placement of Jackson's corps on the high ground overlooking the west bank of the Rappahannock River to the south of the army's First Corps, which had occupied the heights behind the town not ten days before and was under the command of Lieutenant General James Longstreet.

This had become necessary, Lee told Jackson, because the move to the south of the Army of the Potomac towards Fredericksburg was a threat to the capital city of Richmond. The Northern army had started its march under its beloved commander, the dapper General George B. McClellan, only to see him suddenly replaced by Major General Ambrose E. Burnside, one of his corps chiefs.

So Jackson's threefold mission would be to support Longstreet, extend the right, and guard that flank.

The pleasant old town of Fredericksburg upon which two armies were converging, lay on the west bank of the Rappahannock where the river made almost a right-angle turn of direction from due east to southeast on its way to the broad waters of Chesapeake Bay. Guarded on the west by the hills upon which now rested the Southern army, it looked across the stream to the Stafford Heights where were gathered the thousand on thousand of Federal troops warily eyeing their enemies in gray.

Burnside, their handsome commander with his hirsute adornment which has since worked its way into the English language, was unsure of himself in the role of commanding general. He had reluctantly taken over the job, replacing his good friend McClellan, finally sacked by

President Lincoln because of his uncertainty and inde-
cisiveness in conducting combat operations.

When he had assumed command, only a relatively small
Confederate force was on guard at Fredericksburg. So
Burnside decided he would strike south, cross the Rap-
pahannock at the old colonial city, then move swiftly to-
wards Richmond, forcing Lee to give battle in front of the
Southern capital.

It was a good plan if he was quick enough.

But he was opposing a master of the art of war.

Almost as if he were reading Burnside's mind, Lee had
begun to strengthen the small outpost at Fredericksburg.
In short order Longstreet's corps was ordered north, with
Jackson alerted to be prepared to cross the mountains to
join the main forces.

So when Burnside's advanced units reached Falmouth
on the north side of the river across from Fredericksburg,
they could see Lee's soldiers gathering on the other side.

There was still time to effect a crossing but Burnside was
unlucky in other ways.

When his troops arrived at Falmouth they found that the
materiel and engineers needed to throw pontoon bridges
across the river were not there. So they waited.

They waited for four and a half days.

This was a very dangerous thing to do in front of the
Army of Northern Virginia.

But Burnside would not change his plans.

He would thrown his pontoon bridges across the Rappahannock.

He would storm through Fredericksburg.

He would defeat Lee.

It was a tall order.

2

Two Guns for
Burnside

S HORTLY BEFORE THREE O'CLOCK ON THE COLD MORNING
of December 11, 1862, Burnside's pontoon trains were
driven to the river bank where his engineers were waiting
to begin their work. A last quarter moon reflected its faint
glow off the surface of the Rappahannock.

The men toiled silently, sliding the huge pontoon boats
into the water where they would be decked over with
wooden planking in preparation for their dangerous proj-
ection toward the farther shore. At the same time the
attacking columns of infantry which would cross over the
bridges were on the move.

16

They were protected not only by the blackness of the night but by a fog gathering over the river.

On the other side Confederate eyes and ears were straining to confirm the opening moves of the assault on their river fortress. But nothing could be seen.

Then about five o'clock, Colonel John C. Fiser of the Seventeenth Mississippi, on guard in front of the town, felt he could wait no longer, for the sounds of the pontoon bridge builders indicated they were nearing the Fredericksburg shore.

Although nothing of the enemy could yet be seen, he ordered his infantry to open fire.

It was then that the double crash of the signal guns roared out the call to action to the waiting Southern army.

The Battle of Fredericksburg had begun.

Exposed as they were to the galling rifle fire, the bridge builders in front of the town were forced to retreat to their own side from time to time, bringing their dead and wounded with them.

For the Federal effort to throw two more pontoon bridges about a mile downstream of the town, it was a different story. Here the Southern lines drew away from the river. So in the fog and the darkness two bridges were thrown and the United States Army crossed the Rappahannock.

All the long morning the Confederate infantry in the town successfully frustrated the bridging efforts before Fredericksburg, until Burnside at the urging of his artillery commander, General Henry J. Hunt, ordered the pontoon boats to be used to ferry the troops across the river. This was done early in the afternoon following a roaring artillery bombardment on the Southern lines.

The bridges were then laid.

By nightfall the Federal host was across the Rappahannock preparing to draw its battle lines for the coming assaults.

Meanwhile Jackson was moving the Second Corps onto the ridge line extending south from Longstreet's positions back of the town.

The morning of the 12th dawned with heavy haze obscuring the river valley as it had done the day before. There was little action during the day as both antagonists spent the hours feeling out the dispositions of each other.

Lee made a long reconnaissance of his right where he determined the main attack would fall. In this he was correct for Burnside had ordered his Left Grand Division commander, General William B. Franklin, to use all his force to get into Lee's right rear while his Right Grand Division, under General Edwin V. Sumner, pinned Longstreet to the hills behind the town.

The Southern commander also used the respite to call in his detached units which had been guarding the over-extended right flank reaching far down the river. Overall the Army of Northern Virginia was spread out over a front of twenty miles. It was time to shorten the lines.

Still Lee found it hard to believe that Burnside was preparing to throw his magnificent army of 125,000 of all ranks against his own 78,000 graycoats in their rifle pits, supported by three hundred and six guns in the artillery positions. It would be a slaughterhouse.

Yet he had to trust his own eyes and prepare for the storm to come.

That storm was gathering in the thousands of bluecoats already across the Rappahannock and continuing to pour across the pontoon bridges from the farther side.

A freezing night came down on the embattled lines, made colder by a cutting wind and a strange ground fog rising from old snow spots scattered about the fields where the soldiers made ready for the morrow.

3

The Bloody Hours

LEE WAS ABOUT EARLY THE MORNING OF DECEMBER 13, riding through the predawn darkness, made more obscure by the chilling fog which lay heavily over the valley of the Rappahannock.

He was bound for his observation post which he had established on a rise about a mile and one-half southwest of the town, within Longstreet's lines. This spot, after the quick ways of war, was already known as Lee's Hill.

From here about seventeen minutes after seven, he could see a red sun rising over the Federal's left flank. But of the enemy, hidden by the river fog, he could see nothing, although the murmur of voices, the call of bugles and drums, and even some band music, attested to his presence.

After a while his corps commanders, Longstreet and Jackson, and other general officers rode up to report and compare conditions on the various sectors fronting their commands. In all, they were satisfied with the strength of the position.

Jackson, attired in a new uniform coat, the gift ot cavalry commander "Jeb" Stuart, was all for attacking under cover of the fog before the Army of the Potomac could launch its assaults.

But Lee would have none of it.

He would stand where they were, letting the enemy wear itself out in hopeless attacks.

Longstreet, even then evolving his theories of the power of the tactical defensive, was more than satisfied with the army's position. And well he might be, for when the Federal columns debouched out of the town to attack the Confederate left anchored on Marye's Heights, they faced gradually rising ground broken by a sunken road with stone retaining walls affording perfect cover for the waiting Confederate infantry. From the heights above, their advance would be exposed to artillery fire almost all the way.

By ten o'clock the fogs and mists were beginning to clear away, revealing minute by minute more of the details of the vast blue host mustered on the plain below the Confederate positions. The sight took the breath away.

Jackson estimated fifty-five thousand infantry and countless guns before him on the right, while thousands more were gathered in the ruined streets of the town preparing for their assault on Longstreet.

Lee decided the action was about to begin.

Quietly he ordered: "Test the ranges on the left."

Shortly a flame of artillery fire roared northward from Marye's Heights to the bend of the river.

As if on signal, Federal infantry in great force began

advancing toward the ground held by A. P. Hill of Jackson's corps where it joined Longstreet's right. Almost immediately they were halted by enfilading fire from their left, delivered by guns of Pelham's horse artillery, and did not continue their march until the Rebel battery had been driven off.

They then continued their deployment to extend the Federal left in flawless fashion. Lee watched in professional admiration at the execution of the movement not knowing that it was commanded by General George Gordon Meade, a brother engineer officer and companion-at-arms in the Old Army in the Mexican War. They would meet again under more fateful circumstances.

When they were ready, the long blue lines began their advance across the plain towards the Southern position. But Hill withheld his fire so the movement continued towards the higher ground in drill field fashion. Onwards they came until the gunners could hardly restrain their impatience.

How long would they have to wait?

Almost on the moment, the shouted orders were passed from battery to battery, the last commands lost in the roar of the first salvo.

The Federal line wavered under the fire.

But still they came on.

A second and third salvo settled the matter.

It was too much!

Slowly and in good order, the long blue lines retired to gather themselves for another try.

When the first advance had been launched against Jackson, Longstreet ordered his artillery to open on his own front to further engage the enemy and prevent it from concentrating on the right flank.

The shells rained down on Fredericksburg, the pontoon bridges, and wherever the blue army showed itself. From his commanding position, "Old Pete," as his soldiers called him, could regard with great satisfaction the natural strength of the ground which he held.

It was such that he, along with Lee, felt it hard to believe that Burnside would attack him head-on. In this he was shortly to be disabused.

From the ruins of the town the blue columns emerged to complete their deployment at the foot of the slope leading upwards to the sunken road and the Confederate artillery emplacements above.

The commands rang down the lines.

The troops lowered their heads and charged.

The mixed artillery and infantry fire which met them staggered the assault. Nothing human could stand before it. They had to fall back to the line of the ditch where they had started.

As on the right, the Federal attack had failed.

The bloody noon was near its end.

But not this battle.

Meade, heavily reinforced, was preparing a second and more powerful attack on Jackson's lines.

It was preceded by a savage artillery bombardment smashing at the Confederate guns along the entire Southern line from the bend in the river on the north to the far south flank where "Jeb" Stuart's cavalrymen were covering for Jackson.

In the midst of the fire storm, Meade sent his men forward, aiming for some boggy woodland which pointed like an arrow towards the center of Jackson's position. At first they were halted momentarily by the ferocity of the Southern artillery fire, but gathering themselves, the blue-coats came roaring in until they had penetrated the targeted woodland, driving the defenders before them. From his observation post, Lee could see that his right was being threatened by disaster.

What had gone wrong?

Fragmentary reports from the field told of a gap which had been left virtually undefended because it was believed the boggy woods were an impassable obstacle.

Watching anxiously through his field glasses, Lee could see Confederate prisoners being taken into the Federal lines.

Would Burnside break through Jackson's Second Corps?

His answer came in strange sounds shrilling above the roar of artillery and musketry. In an instant he knew the damage had been repaired. It was the old fox hunter's cry, now the trademark of the Army of Northern Virginia, the famous Rebel Yell.

Now he could see bluecoats breaking out of the woods, fleeing for safety to their own lines.

Watching his troops coming hard on their heels, Lee's fighting blood took control.

He turned to Longstreet who stood with him.

"It is well that war is so terrible—we should grow too fond if it!"

With these words both he and Longstreet had to turn their attention to their immediate front, the long bloody slope of Marye's Hill, where the Confederate infantry from the protection of the walls of the sunken road, had just repelled another attack from the ditch in front of the town.

Lee could see the Federals massing for yet another and heavier assault.

Voicing his fears that they might effect a breakthrough, he got his answer from Longstreet: "General, if you put every man on the other side of the Potomac on that field to approach me over the same line, and give me plenty of ammunition, I will kill them all before they reach my line. Look to your right; you are in some danger there, but not on my line."

What Lee could not know, and what perhaps Longstreet

himself did not understand, was that these defiant words represented a deeply held conviction that a strong defense would always prevail over a strong offense, all else being equal.

It was the statement of a dogmatic belief which might produce far reaching effects on another field.

But the two generals had no time for philosophy that afternoon on the heights above Fredericksburg, for Burnside was continuing to throw wave after wave of blue-clad infantrymen at the unassailable position.

The dead piled up on top of each other until about seven o'clock in the evening when the futile wastage came to an end.

4

Northern Lights on a Ghastly Field

NIGHT CAME DOWN BLACK AND COLD ON THE BLOODY field.

Cries of the wounded rose in piteous entreaty for aid.

The two armies, exhausted by the day of killing, lay on their arms, grateful for even a brief respite.

Then far in the north the night was coming alive.

A pale rose spread across the sky, deepening suddenly to a dark red to match the blood stains in the fields.

Shifting shafts of frosty white were moving ghostlike across the skies.

It was the every changing aurora borealis, fading and brightening while its spectral glow illuminated the faces of the wondering soldiers.

Riding back to his headquarters under the exotic celestial display, Lee felt confident that Burnside would renew his assaults in the morning, affording him an opportunity to administer a crushing defeat on the Northern army after which he would move to the offensive and the complete destruction of the foe.

All but one of his generals were in agreement: Burnside had too much at stake to quit now.

Meanwhile the entrenchment work went on through the night, further strengthening the defensive power of the long lines.

But when the heavy river fog dissipated on the morning of the fourteenth, it became apparent there would be no attacks by Burnside that morning. The enemy continued inactive throughout the rest of that day and the next.

What Lee could not know was that when Burnside proposed to mount new assaults on the strong Confederate positions, all of his generals advised against any further attacks.

So the fourteenth dragged on into the fifteenth without major action.

When a perplexed Lee rode out in the darkness of December 16th, he made for the right and Jackson's corps.

It was a rainy morning with heavy fog again obscuring the valley and the river.

Anxiously he and Jackson made their way to a lookout point only to be informed that the enemy had gone.

Gone?

It was. true.

Hidden by the night and fog, the great blue host had pulled back across the river in a soundless maneuver aided by a wind blowing away from the Southern lines.

At a cost of more than 12,000 casualties, Burnside had been forced to abandon his attack on Lee.

The great battle was over.

5

Fredericksburg Falls Silent

THE FALLOUT FROM THE FEDERAL DISASTER AT FREDER-icksburg was immense and scattered in all directions.
President Lincoln, whose Republican Party had sustained severe losses in state elections in the autumn of 1862, got the bad news, not from his own War Department, but, from the New York *Tribune's* war correspondent, Henry Villard, fresh from the battlefield. When Villard had spoken of disaster, Lincoln had shaken his head sadly, saying: "I hope it is not so bad as all that."

On December 30, Quartermaster General M. C. Meigs wrote Burnside: "Exhaustion steals over the country. Confidence and hope are dying. . . . I begin to doubt the possibility of maintaining the contest beyond this winter, unless the popular heart is encouraged by victory on the Rappahannock."

Fears of foreign intervention, particularly by Great Britain on the part of the South, rose in Washington.

Generals Burnside, Sumner and Franklin, would leave the Army of the Potomac, not to rejoin during the campaign.

If Washington was engulfed with a mood of despair, Richmond was exultant.

The newspapers crowed, the people and the churches gave thanks, and some in the administration of the Confederacy were confident that the war would soon end in victory.

Lee did not share this euphoria.

All he could see was more hard fighting in the months ahead.

In the midst of the success at Fredericksburg he had explored ways of exploiting the great victory. But he had finally to conclude that he could not expose the Army of Northern Virginia to destruction before the Federal artillery arrayed on the Stafford Heights across the Rappahannock.

It had been a difficult decision but Lee was a soldier.

When winter gave over to spring, he knew his army must be on the offensive again. The South just could not afford to relinquish the initiative to the enemy.

To do so would be the beginning of the end.

Jackson, cut from the same mold, had not wanted to give battle at Fredericksburg because the position restricted opportunity for maneuver.

With Longstreet it was another story.

He had gloried in the strength of his dispositions on the hills behind the town.

For him Fredericksburg had been the perfect battle.

Part II

How Can We Get at These People?
   —Lee to Jackson, May 1, 1863

Battle of Chancellorsville. End of the Battle.

6

The Bacon Hunter

SEVERE WINTER WEATHER HAMPERED THE MOVEMENTS OF both armies around Fredericksburg during the first month of the bloody year of 1863, with Lee using the respite to further fortify his lines along the Rappahannock on both sides of the ruined town. Burnside, still in command, made a few futile gestures with his troops, but in the end nothing came of it all.

Meanwhile Lee had learned of heavy Federal troop movements in transports south on Chesapeake Bay to Hampton Roads at the mouth of the James River. From there, this force at corps strength could move against Richmond or into eastern North Carolina. With his own front inactive, Lee answered a call for troops for the Confederate capital by sending first Pickett's, then Hood's division of Longstreet's First Corps.

Shortly thereafter Longstreet followed in command. Along with his own divisions, "Old Pete" was to command the Department of Virginia and North Carolina, with the additional task of securing the ample supplies of foodstuffs available in the eastern counties of North Carolina.

Lee placed but one restriction on the use of Hood's and Pickett's divisions. They must always be close enough to the railroad to be available for rapid return to the Rappahannock line in case of a major Northern offensive.

Longstreet, for his part, was soon urging Lee to send him the other two divisions of his First Corps to facilitate the gathering in of the hogs, corn and fish available in the region. He went so far as to once suggest that Lee could hold the Rappahannock front with Jackson's corps when his own troops were sent south.

All this was done without rancor of any kind.

But it did show that Longstreet, enjoying the exercise of independent command, was also coming to regard himself as a strategist equal, if not superior, to Lee.

Meanwhile the Army of the Potomac had acquired a new commander in the person of Major General Joseph "Fighting Joe" Hooker who had commanded Burnside's Center Grand Division at Fredericksburg. Ambitious with a rough and sometimes boastful tongue, he was a good administrator who rapidly restored the fighting powers of his troops.

With winter sliding into spring, he decided the time had come to put his 138,000 troops into action.

Across the river, Lee with 62,500 men of all arms, waited to frustrate his aims.

In the black predawn hours of April 29 Lee was awakened to learn that Hooker was crossing the Rappahannock.

The spring campaign had begun.

7

Hooker Saddles Up

Reports of the Rappahannock crossing which brought Lee out of a sound sleep that April morning had to do with a pontoon bridge being thrown across the river in the darkness and the fog, unobserved by the Confederate pickets. He was told the enemy was huddled under shelter of the river bank, making no attempt to advance.

Suspect of the inactivity, as indicating a feinting thrust with the blow to fall elsewhere, he had Jackson post his troops along the hills which had so bloodily repelled the Federals in December.

He did not have long to wait for confirmation of his doubts.

A dispatch from Jeb Stuart, watching the Rappahannock

fords some twenty miles to the west, reported a large force of infantry accompanied by artillery and cavalry had crossed the river and were making for the fords of the Rapidan in the direction of the melancholy country crossroads of Chancellorsville, presided over by the old, pillared Chancellor's House, deep in the grimly forbidding, cut-over country known as the Wilderness.

This would put the enemy directly in Lee's rear, from where if he had the power, Hooker could crush the Confederates against the other Federal force, even now across the Rappahannock in front of Fredericksburg.

This is exactly what Hooker had planned.

With tremendous force, he had crossed the Rappahannock and Rapidan west of Fredericksburg in Lee's rear, leaving the wholly competent Major General John Sedgwick and his two corps to keep Lee and Jackson busy on the Fredericksburg front.

Hooker was in high spirits at Chancellorsville the morning of May 1 as he put his four corps in motion towards the east and Lee's rear.

He was not the only one.

Corps commander George Gordon Meade burst through his usually cold reserve to shout to a fellow officer: "Hurrah for old Joe! We're on Lee's flank and he doesn't know it."

But Lee did know.

He already had troops digging in in front of Chancellorsville and he was preparing to send Jackson marching to that ill-omened crossroads, leaving the caustic-tongued Jubal Early with 10,000 men to face John Sedgwick's 47,000 before Fredericksburg.

With his troops stirring in the midnight hours of May Day, Jackson and his staff rode out in the lead of the long long column on the Plank Road headed into the ominous Wilderness and the fateful crossroads of Chancellorsville.

It was a pleasant march, lustrous moonlight bathing the high-spirited infantry as they moved easily through the open farming country behind the hills of Fredericksburg.

Moonset at dawn found them enwrapped in dense cooling mists which dissipated under the rays of the warming sun.

It was a perfect May Day.

About 8 A.M. Jackson rode up to where Anderson's division of the First Corps, which had been dispatched by Lee to guard the western approaches, was running a line of entrenchments across the roads leading out of the Wilderness.

Old Jack studied the ground to his front. Then quickly made up his mind.

Issuing rapid-fire orders to Anderson to mass his division for an advance into the Wilderness up the Old Turnpike towards Chancellorsville with his left flank units using the parallel Plank Road, Jackson would send his own Second Corps in their trace.

It was about eleven o'clock.

The transition from defense to the offense had been swift.

Action was equally swift in coming, with rifle and artillery fire announcing that Hooker's Federals were in the Wilderness in force and were fighting back.

As this action was developing, Jackson met Lee and his staff riding up from Fredericksburg.

Amidst the cheering of their troops Lee and Jackson rode to the left where the skirmishing was growing hotter. But Lee had no suggestions for his chief lieutenant and shortly took his leave to ride off to the right towards the Rappahannock where he found the Federal lines drawn in while well supported by their artillery.

It was a cut-up country with small swamps and gray thickets.

Riding back to the Plank Road, he rejoined Jackson in the fading daylight to report there was no opportunity for attack on the Federal left.

While the two generals canvassed other possible courses of action, two engineer officers were sent out to explore opportunities to the Confederate front.

Three miles to the west into the Wilderness, Joe Hooker, standing on the steps of the Chancellor's House, had undergone a strange change of heart.

Instead of an irresistible advance which would pin Lee up against Sedgwick, he was talking about the strong defensive position he now held.

His senior major general, Darius Couch, could hardly believe his ears when Hooker told him: "It's all right, Couch, I've got Lee just where I want him; he must fight me on my own ground."

The grizzled veteran commander of the II Corps who had gone to army headquarters to protest the order to go over to the defense, walked away shaking his head, leaving the soldiers of Hooker's Army of the Potomac throwing up field fortifications in the growing shadows.

8

To Turn a Flank

LEE AND JACKSON, AWAITING THE RETURN OF THEIR ENGI-
neers who were surveying the immediate front,
continued their discussion under the bright moonlight
while sitting on a fallen log.

Jackson was still of his original opinion that Hooker,
because of his easy retirement to positions in front of
Chancellorsville, was preparing to pull his army back
across the river. His movement "either a feint or a failure,"
as Stonewall put it.

Lee shook his head in disagreement, contending
Hooker had committed too much to his advance to abandon it now.

So the two generals sat talking when Jeb Stuart dismounted to report intelligence of major import.

General Fitz Lee had discovered that the Federal right west of Chancellorsville was in the air, having no natural defensive terrain on which to anchor its line.

Because Lee suspected that no opportunities would be offered against Hooker's heavily fortified lines hidden in the threatening shadows to the Southern front, and if no attack could be delivered on the Federal left flank, what would be the chances on their right?

Now Stuart was telling him there was a chance.

What about roads leading towards that flank through the tangled Wilderness?

Stuart said he would find out and rode off.

It was close on to midnight when the two engineers returned from their careful reconnaissance of Hooker's front.

Lee was correct.

It was too strong to be attacked.

That left only Hooker's right.

By the light of a lantern, Lee bent close over the battle map.

Looking up at Jackson, but speaking to himself, it was then he said: "How can we get at those people?"

The silent Jackson bent low, watched Lee's finger roughly trace a route through the Wilderness to and beyond Hooker's right flank, coming to rest at a position from where an attack could be driven down the whole line into the Federal rear.

Lee looked up at the bearded Jackson. "General Stuart will cover your movement with his cavalry."

Old Jack nodded his assent. "My troops will move at four o'clock," he said, and with that he moved away from the campfire to bed down on his saddle-blanket under the trees.

Lee was shortly joined by the Reverend B. T. Lacy of

Jackson's corps who was familiar with that part of the Wilderness. Sent by Stuart, he reported on roads and paths leading off to the west, leaving Lee convinced that the projected flanking march could be made.

He then spread his blankets in the forest.

Before the dawning of May 2, he awoke to find Jackson already standing by the fire studying the map.

Lee asked his most famous lieutenant what he was going to do.

"Go around here," he answered, running his finger along a route drawn by Major Jed Hotchkiss, his topographical engineer. "What do you propose to make this movement with?"

"With my whole corps," Jackson replied.

It was breath-taking.

If he could get in Hooker's rear with 28,000, the blow he would launch would be catastrophic to the Federal army.

A startled Lee looked at him.

"What will you leave me?"

"The divisions of Anderson and McLaws."

These men from Longstreet's First Corps would leave Lee with 14,000 soldiers to face Hooker's force of from 50 to 70 thousand troops.

To hold this host at bay while Jackson led his graycoats on an all-day march across the front of the Army of the Potomac would be a giant task.

But Lee was game.

He nodded his assent.

With that Jackson left to organize the march.

But even with the need for speed, it took just so much time to feed the troops and get them on the road.

So it was about 8 o'clock when the head of the long long column of infantry, artillery and trains turned into the Furnace Road to follow Colonel Tom Munford's Second

Virginia Cavalry towards the southwest. But the delays did not seem to fret Stonewall other than increase his insistence that the troops must "Press on! Press on!"

Then coming to Lee's headquarters near the Catharine Furnace, an ancient iron furnace which had given the road its name, he rode out of the column to exchange a few words with the commanding general.

Watching soldiers could see the blaze of battle in his eyes while he pointed forward with Lee nodding agreement.

Then "Old Blue Light," as his men liked to call him, was back in his place in the endless column, wending its way forward into the mysterious Wilderness.

Lee watched the figure, sitting straight in the saddle, until it was swallowed up in the forest.

Then he turned back to his immediate problem of deceiving the mighty hosts of Meade's, Slocum's and Howard's corps in his front, as to his own strength, and so delude and delay them throughout a long nervous morning and afternoon.

Anderson and McLaws sent their skirmishers far forward to quarrel with the Federals whenever one would show his head. They did their work well for no attack developed on Lee's lines during the anxious hours.

Strangely enough, Hooker's forward lines had caught glimpses of Jackson's column as it swung south, misleading "Fighting Joe" into thinking Lee was in retreat. He ordered the unskillful Daniel Sickles to the attack with his III Corps. But Jackson's rear guard beat it off with ease.

All that resulted was a big gap in Hooker's lines where Sickles' corps had been, further isolating Major General Otis Howard's XI Corps on the far right flank, now the unsuspecting quarry of Jackson's men.

After this flurry of excitement, Stonewall's march continued without incident until suddenly a galloping rider halted before Jackson. It was Fitz Lee of the cavalry.

"General," he said to him privately, "if you will ride with me, halting your columns here, out of sight, I will show you the enemy's right, and you will perceive the great advantage of attacking down the old turnpike instead of the Plank Road, the enemy's lines being taken in reverse. Bring only one courier, as you will be in view from the top of the hill."

When they topped the hill, Jackson could see it all.

There before him were the long lines of Howard's XI Corps. The troops, their arms stacked, were resting at ease, evidently preparing for a leisurely evening meal.

Jackson's lips tightened while the strange blue light blazed in his eyes.

Silently he made his reconnaissance. In five minutes he had it all.

The courier was sent off with orders to the halted troops. Then he and Fitz Lee were riding back.

Once again at the head of the column, he wrote his commanding General:

> Near 3 P.M.
> May 2nd, 1863
>
> General,
> The enemy has made a stand at Chancellor's which is about 2 miles from Chancellorsville. I hope as soon as practicable to attack.
> I trust that an ever kind Providence will bless us with great success.
>
> Respectfully,
> T. J. Jackson
> Lt. Genl.
>
> Genl. R. E. Lee
> The leading division is up and the next two appear to be well-closed.

At almost the same time he received Jackson's note, Lee heard dark news from the Fredericksburg front.

Early had abandoned those strong lines through the passage of wrong verbal orders, and was marching to join Lee before Chancellorsville.

Lee immediately countermanded these erroneous instructions in a note to Early in hopes of salvaging the damage.

More he could not now do.

With but two hours of daylight remaining, the fate of the Army of Northern Virginia was truly in the hands of the gods of war.

9

The Rebel Yell

DRIVING HIS COLUMNS NORTHWARD TOWARDS THE OLD Turnpike, Jackson glanced upwards at the westering sun.

Time now had become the all important factor in the developing attack. His troops must have time for their deployment across the Old Turnpike down which they would move to the east against the unsuspecting flank of the Federal right. Time they would need to develop their assaults. And if they were successful, more time would be needed to exploit them into what he could see had the elements of maybe the South's greatest victory.

"Press on! Press on! Close up! Close up!"

The sweating infantry acknowledged his commands with redoubled efforts.

To each of his division commanders, he carefully explained where he wanted them placed and their objectives after the advance had begun.

Critical points would be two open glades in the Wilderness. First would be the place known as Talley's Farm, then farther to the east another clearing known as Melzi Chancellor's. Hooker's XI Corps line under Howard ran through both of them.

In the shadows of the confusing woodland it took precious minutes to get 28,000 men into their battle lines.

Jackson's battle blood was up, his eyes the piercing color which had earned from his soldiers his title of "Old Blue Light."

He told his staff the order would be to: "Thrust bayonets!"

The skirmish line commander rode up with a bugler.

Jackson took out his watch.

It was fifteen minutes after five o'clock.

He frowned.

There was but one hour and thirty-three minutes of daylight left.

Turning to the commander of his leading division, he asked: "Are you ready General Rodes?"

"Yes, Sir," came the answer.

"You can go forward then," Jackson replied.

Rodes nodded to the skirmish line commander.

Immediately his bugler sounded the stirring notes of "Advance!"

From the right and the left other buglers picked up the call to action to send it reverberating through the darkening thickets of the Wilderness.

The gray lines responded with speed, crashing through the woodland to send frightened deer and rabbits racing toward the still unwarned Federal troops.

A few rifle shots came from the front.

Then realizing that they were in for the kill, they raised the high pitched quavering Rebel Yell. It swept down the long lines, then was picked up and repeated again, and yet again, and again.

"An unearthly, fiendish yell, such as no other troops or civilized beings ever uttered," one Federal chaplain described it.

The startled bluecoats tried to make a stand, but it was too late. Some of the troops started to run, then more and more.

It was panic!

The light fortifications at Talley's Farm went down in the charge.

Onwards Jackson's men swept towards Melzi Chancellor's.

By this time fear was sweeping down Howard's lines. Men were throwing down their arms trying to escape from the doom coming at them from out of the forest. Horses, guns, beef cattle, wagons were all mixed with men in the confused debacle.

Melzi Chancellor's was captured.

Federal officers tried to stem the tide of defeat to no avail.

Hooker's right flank was being folded back upon the center, the tremendous roar of musketry and artillery shattering what had been the calm of the twilight.

Only when the charging Confederate infantry entered the woods beyond Melzi Chancellor's was their surge slowed.

Over the tops of the trees, the rising full moon glowed angry red through the battle smoke.

Yet it did shed faint light to aid the infantry in continuing the attack. But this was proving difficult in the cut-up woodland now made more difficult by the littered debris of defeat.

When Jackson resumed his ride towards the now confused and uncertain front, he found himself overtaken by his senior division commander, Major General Ambrose Powell Hill.

He had but few words for that fiery, impulsive fighter.

"Press them! Cut them off from the United States Ford, Hill! Press them!"

Far across the Wilderness Lee had spent a nervous afternoon, although nothing ruffled his calm demeanor.

He had heard nothing further from Jackson after the 3 P.M. note.

What had happened to the attack?

He had heard nothing more from his rear guard at Fredericksburg.

Was Early being defeated?

Suddenly from out of the west came the growl of quarreling gun fire. It rose rapidly to roaring crescendo.

Lee's staff officers paused to listen.

It must be Jackson!

Lee did not wait.

Let the troops who had been facing the eastern edge of Hooker's penetration now redouble their fire to take the weight off of Jackson's advance. Go up to the point of actual attack, then break it off so no men are lost. This was make-believe but it must look real. Hooker must not be allowed to transfer troops to oppose the flanking movement from the west.

In this subterfuge Lee was entirely successful, for in the night, and the confusion and the chaos, Hooker did not really know what was happening.

The powerful Federal artillery around Chancellorsville sprayed the woodlands in futile salvos but other than listening to the roar of the fighting to the west and the sight of bursting shell in the treetops where the battle was raging, the redlegs could do little to influence the course of the battle.

A bewildered Hooker was near panic himself.

He sent off an urgent dispatch to Sedgwick ordering him to seize Fredericksburg immediately and then head for the Wilderness, attacking and destroying any Rebel forces in his way.

It was a cry for help.

Could Sedgwick comply?

10

Jackson Down

THE BATTLE FURY BOILING WITHIN HIM, JACKSON RODE slowly towards the front. Once his small party of staff aides, couriers and signalmen were forced to stop to seek shelter from a furious cannonade from Federal artillery combing this portion of the Wilderness.

When it ceased the ride forward resumed.

Jackson was determined to destroy Hooker who he sensed would be retreating on the fords back across the Rappahannock when he had learned the immense damage done to his forces. To this end he wished to see for himself the conditions under which he must launch a night attack through the tangled Wilderness.

The party was now out beyond the forward edge of the

48

Confederate picket line. So far, his aides were becoming increasingly nervous over his safety.

One of them asked: "General, don't you think this is the wrong place for you?"

His answer: "The danger is all over—the enemy is routed! Go back and tell A. P. Hill to press right on!"

Little could be seen in the darkness of the forest other than the moonlight shining down upon the Plank Road. But up ahead Jackson and his guide heard axmen felling trees and officers shouting to their men. They could go no farther.

Jackson turned back to put his own troops in motion for the final blow.

Suddenly several shots were fired out of the forest.

Then a volley of fire flamed out of the night.

The commanding voice of A. P. Hill split the darkness. "Cease firing! Cease firing!"

Jackson's frightened horse, the famed Little Sorrel, bolted into the woods.

"Cease firing!" one of Jackson's own aides shouted. "You are firing into your own men!"

He was answered back. "Who gave that order? It's a lie! Pour it into them, boys!"

Instantly a blaze of rifle fire shattered the night.

Jackson was hit twice, once in his left shoulder and again in his right hand.

Out of the control of his rider, Little Sorrel headed for enemy lines. A bough nearly knocked the general off the horse as he fought for control of the reins. The wounded Stonewall did manage to get Little Sorrel headed back towards the Confederate front.

Before he could faint and fall, two officers on either side of him brought horse and rider to a stand. They passed Jackson to the ground as Hill dismounted to kneel by his fallen chief.

"Is the wound painful?" he asked.

"Very," Jackson answered, "my arm is broken."

A litter was brought up as a Federal unit threatened to attack from the front.

Leaping to his feet, Hill went off to rally his troops. As he left he told Jackson he would attempt to keep his wounding from the men.

The wounded general thanked him.

When Hill was preparing the line, there came a flurry of fire and Hill was lashed across his boot tops. How badly hurt? he asked himself, only to find that he could stand but not walk.

He could not command the corps.

The next senior major general, Jeb Stuart, must take over, so an officer was dispatched on a wild ride to find the cavalry commander. At the same time the corps' right wing repulsed a disorganized Federal night attack.

All the while the shriek and roar of artillery shells enveloped the small group gathered around the wounded lieutenant general who now was being carried to the rear. After transfer to an army ambulance for the slow journey to the corps field hospital at long last Jackson arrived shortly after eleven.

After examination of his wounds, the surgeons prepared for the operation which would require the amputation of his left arm as well as removal of the musket ball in his right hand. The surgery went well and at long last Jackson could get some rest.

Finally when the artillery fire over the Wilderness began to subside on towards midnight, Lee to the south of Chancellorsville went off to catch some sleep. But not for long.

He was wakened about half past two by the arrival at headquarters of Jackson's chief signal officer who had been with the general when they had been fired upon by their own troops. Lee rejoiced at the news of the great victory on the Federal right, but he moaned sadly when told of Jackson's wounding and the transfer of command first to Hill, then to Rodes, and finally to Stuart.

But the battle would not wait.

Instructions were drafted for the new commander:

May 3, 1863—3 A.M.

General:

It is necessary that the glorious victory thus far achieved be prosecuted with the utmost vigor, and the enemy given no time to rally. As soon, therefore, as it is possible, they must be pressed, so that we may unite the two wings of the army.

Endeavor, therefore, to dispossess them of Chancellorsville, which will permit the union of the whole army.

I shall myself proceed to join you as soon as I can make arrangements on this side, but let nothing delay the completion of the plan of driving the enemy from his rear and from his positions.

I shall give orders that every effort be made on this side at daybreak to aid in the junction.

Lee then prepared his forces for the attack which would unite the army

11

The Long Arm Speaks

ANXIOUSLY WAITING FOR DAYLIGHT, THE DASHING, ROMAN-tic young cavalryman, who had never directed infantry in battle, Jeb Stuart called for his acting artillery commander to spot positions for the guns while he rode the line to ready the attack.

Because the Confederate line bent back westward on its right, the first assaults were launched from there with the almost immediate capture of a cleared hill called Hazel Grove along with four pieces of Federal artillery which were in place there.

As soon as the graycoats swept onwards towards Chancellorsville, their own batteries were emplacing on the captured hill. It indeed was to prove a most valuable prize.

But the infantry were having a difficult time in advancing their lines through the tangled woodland.

Federal field fortifications of logs and earth did not make their task easier.

In fact, by seven o'clock the front and center of the corps had been forced back by the Yankee infantry, exposing the left flank units which now were being subjected to savage attacks. They too began to falter so the entire Confederate line was in peril.

It was then the Rebel guns on Hazel Grove spoke out.

The massed artillery began throwing very heavy fire against the Federal flank.

The Southern cannon also ranged in on a knoll named Fairview in front of Chancellorsville where the Northern artillery was in place.

While the Rebel gunners yelled in glee, they watched their shells exploding amidst the enemy batteries. With a decline in the Federal fire, they redoubled their efforts to see Union cannon pulling out of their exposed position.

Now through the smoke coiling over the battle lines they could see the Yankee infantry wavering under the weight of the Confederate shells.

More yells and more fire!

Fairview itself was being abandoned by the Northern artillerymen.

The thirty guns on Hazel Grove fired ever faster.

One Rebel cannonball scored a direct hit on a pillar in front of the Chancellorsville mansion against which "Fighting Joe" Hooker was lounging, watching the exchange of shell fire. Stunned, he was knocked sprawling in the dust.

In the frenzied fury of the fight, Lee, who was directing the First Corps units approaching from the south, could sense the battle was near its climax.

About ten o'clock he rode up on Stuart's right flank division and ordered it to attack in the direction of Fairview

The army was united once more but for the beleaguered Early at Fredericksburg.

12

Cheers and Tears

WHILE LEE SAT ASTRIDE HIS GRAY WARHORSE TRAVELLER at Hazel Grove, he learned that Chancellorsville had been captured.

So through the roar and fire of the dying battle he rode down the Plank Road towards the fateful crossroads.

Much of the forest was on fire, wreathing smoke plumes high above the thickets and glades littered with the debris of war. The wounded and the dead were everywhere, surrounded by castoff rifles, blankets, cartridge boxes, mess gear and all the everyday necessities of the soldier on campaign.

Passing the knoll of Fairview, he could see his Confederate gunners still lobbing shells at the retreating blue regiments.

Then he was entering the clear space of Chancellorsville, the sprawling, many chimneyed mansion burning fiercely under the May sun of high noon.

Confederate troops were crowding their way forward.

It was then they saw him!

Wild cheers hailed his great victory!

Soldiers crowded round him and his famous mount.

With voices hoarse with excitement, they were paying him the greatest tribute they could bestow. These were his men! Soldiers of the Army of Northern Virginia!

Modestly he acknowledged their accolade.

He was then handed a note from the wounded Jackson congratulating him upon the victory.

Quickly he signed a message in return: "General—I have just received your note, informing me that you were wounded. I can only express my regret at the occurrence. Could I have directed events, I would have chosen for the good of the country to be disabled in your stead.

"I congratulate you upon the victory, which is due to your skill and energy."

Before he could issue orders for renewal of the attack on the beaten Hooker, Lee received more bad news.

Sedgwick was across the Rappahannock and had captured the Marye's Heights behind Fredericksburg where Longstreet had made his famous defensive stand in December.

There was nothing else to do, but hold Hooker where he was and send reinforcements to Early.

About five o'clock the sound of a heavy engagement to the east told Lee that his reinforcements had found the enemy.

Sedgwick's march on Lee's rear had been halted at a place named Salem Church. Stuart rode up to his modest bivouac at dark and the pair reviewed the day's battle.

At midnight Lee sought some sleep.

Up before dawn, he sent orders to remove Jackson to a place of safety in the rear.

An early morning reconnaissance revealed that Hooker had greatly strengthened his lines during the night but showed no signs of going over to the offensive.

So detaching even more troops to aid Early repel the VI Corps, he decided he would ride back to supervise the operation.

He did not like what he found. Losing his temper at the slowness of the commanders and their units, he ordered a night attack, so ending the historic fourth of May.

The fifth of May found Sedgwick back north of the Rappahannock, so Lee prepared to resume his assault on Hooker.

But it was to no end.

Hooker too had fled north.

So ended one of the classic battles of history, when Lee, outnumbered by better than two and one-half to one, had totally defeated the Army of the Potomac.

There was another interested party.

In the capital city of Washington, President Abraham Lincoln read a dispatch from Hooker's chief of staff, Brigadier General Daniel Butterfield, while standing in a White House bedroom. It told of the great defeat and included an estimate of casualties. Lincoln's cheeks matched the pale gray color of the stylish paper on the walls.

By mid-day of the sixth of May, Lee started the army back to its old camps around Fredericksburg. It was an easy march but for pelting rain which swept the long columns before darkness fell.

Orders of congratulations to the troops were published the following day, marking the end of the spring campaign.

It had ended in triumph.

Jackson's chaplain called at headquarters to report the general had taken a turn for the worse. Pneumonia was feared.

Lee was distressed at the news. But ever hopeful, he said to the chaplain: "Give Jackson my affectionate regards, and tell him to make haste and get well, and come back to me as soon as he can. He has lost his left arm, but I have lost my right."

The next day, a Sunday which Lee had denoted a day of thanksgiving for the great victory, the news from Jackson's bedside was not good.

Lee who had been long on his knees praying for the life of his greatest lieutenant could not believe it.

For the sake of the destiny of the South, this matchless captain of battle must live.

It was not to be.

After a long courageous fight, he died.

Part III

Select your ground and make the enemy attack you.

—Napoleon

13

To the North

In the days following the death of Jackson, Lee wrestled with two problems of vast portent to the future of the Confederate States of America.

First—What should be done to fill the great void in the army's high command left by the death of Jackson?

Second—What strategy should govern the employment of the Army of Northern Virginia in the immediate months ahead?

Two weeks after the end of the Battle of Chancellorsville, Lee presented his proposed solution to the first problem to Jefferson Davis, his President, in Richmond, Virginia.

First was reshaping the entire command structure so that instead of the old two-corps organization, a new corps would be created to become the Third Corps.

This would greatly facilitate conduct of combat operations as well as streamline administration of the army when it was in the rear areas. Lee had long considered the old two-corps organization excessively cumbersome in combat for the large number of troops in each corps was difficult for a single commander to control.

To lead the newly constituted corps, Lee had three proposals for Davis to consider.

First Corps would continue under that battle-tested veteran of many fields, Lieutenant General James Longstreet. His combat qualities were well known to Lee but there were some newly developing traits of character of which the commanding general seemed unaware.

Second Corps, which had been Jackson's, would now be commanded by Stonewall's trusted lieutenant of the Valley Campaigns, Richard Stoddert Ewell, who loved combat but, unknown to Lee, would always seek the advice of others if it were available on a major battle decision.

Third Corps command would go to the redoubtable Ambrose Powell Hill, whose division was generally credited with being the best in the army. Hill had been a star on several fields, the most prominent being his fortunate appearance in his red battle shirt at the head of his division at exactly the right moment to save Lee's right wing at Antietam. At Chancellorsville he had taken over command of the Second Corps for a short while after Jackson's wounding before being wounded himself.

Jeb Stuart was so invaluable to Lee as his intelligence officer that his transfer to corps command was not considered, so he would continue as commander of the cavalry of the army.

With these matters settled, Lee turned to the greater problem.

Where should the army march next?

General Joe Johnston was being heavily pressed by General U. S. Grant before Vicksburg. Secretary of War Seddon favored sending reinforcements to this front.

Longstreet urged that Braxton Bragg be strengthened in Tennessee by detachments from his own corps.

But Lee told President Davis he could agree with neither, because, he said: "It would be folly to have divided my army; the armies of the enemy were too far apart for me to attempt to fall upon them in detail. I considered the problem in every possible phase, and to my mind, it resolved itself into a choice of one of two things—either to retire to Richmond and stand a siege, which must ultimately have ended in surrender, or to invade Pennsylvania."

So north it was to be.

But he had one opponent.

Longstreet would not give up. He still argued for sending heavy detachments from the army to reinforce Bragg in Tennessee.

Lee listened politely but he would not be moved.

Longstreet then tried to get Lee to agree with him that if the army entered the north it should make its stand on strong ground, inviting the enemy to attack.

Lee listened, but again he would not be moved.

But Longstreet did not listen.

The memories of that unforgettable day at Fredericksburg with the Federal generals shattering their blue columns against the Southern guns obsessed him.

So he convinced himself that he had convinced his commander.

He would enter the North in a most unfortunate frame of mind.

14

Ominous Baggage on the March

WHILE LEE WAS PONDERING HIS INVASION OF THE North, word came on the second of June that Federal forces on the lower peninsula, which had posed a threat to Richmond, were moving northward.

Lee's reaction was immediate.

At a conference at which Longstreet again argued the benefits of a strategic offensive and a tactical defensive, "Old Bald Head," as Ewell was known to his troops, was given instructions to take the Second Corps through Chester Gap in the Blue Ridge to Front Royal and thence down the Shenandoah Valley to Winchester, en route to a crossing of the Potomac at Williamsport.

A. P. Hill's Third corps troops would take over the

Fredericksburg line facing Hooker, which he would hold while the First and Second Corps began the advance into Pennsylvania.

On June 6 with Hooker showing little stomach for another attack on Fredericksburg, Lee moved his own headquarters to Culpeper where he found Longstreet and Ewell's corps preparing for their march north.

Upon his arrival, he was invited by Jeb Stuart to a grand review of all the cavalry to be held the next day. Former colonel of cavalry that he had been in the Old Army, Lee was quick to accept and enjoyed the spectacle staged by his mounted arm.

But the very next morning, show business became real when General Alfred Pleasanton's cavalry corps of the Army of the Potomac surprised the Confederate horse at Brandy Station, almost defeating them before being driven off by an embarrassed Stuart. Although the Southerners held the field at the finish, a humiliated Stuart would enter the new campaign determined to restore his bruised reputation.

So another of Lee's lieutenants would be carrying unneeded mental baggage on the march to the north.

Longstreet's task in the unfolding movement would be to advance on the eastern side of the Blue Ridge thereby covering A. P. Hill's evacuation of the Fredericksburg positions to follow in trace of Ewell into the Shenandoah Valley and thence northward.

Old Pete's Third Corps would then follow on, bringing up the rear of the army as it moved into the fertile and fruited fields of the North.

By June 14 Ewell's Second Corps stood before Winchester in the Valley where Federal General Robert Milroy had from six to eight thousand troops. A sudden and well conducted assault bagged most of them and Ewell had a clear path to the north.

So far so good.

Hooker had not been entirely misled by these maneuvers.

He wanted to take a crack at Lee, but discredited by the Chancellorsville disaster, Washington kept him on a tight leash. He had become merely a caretaker general.

So little by little he edged his army northward but nowhere as far or as fast as Lee's troops were moving.

By June 16 Rodes' division of Ewell's Second Corps was across the Potomac and in Maryland at the river town of Williamsport. There he was ordered to halt and wait until the rest of the corps came up. His cavalry, however, were already far in the van, headed for Pennsylvania.

Ewell himself hurried them on, partly from horseback, partly from a buggy, for he had lost a leg at the Second Manassas or Bull Run.

His swift and decisive handling of the Second Corps on this critical advance made it seem to the soldiers that the spirit of Old Jack must be riding with Ewell.

Of this, only time could determine.

15

Where is Stuart?

BONE WEARY AFTER A SERIES OF CAVALRY CLASHES HAD turned back the Federal troopers from the passes through the Blue Ridge into the Shenandoah Valley through which the Confederate army was passing on its march to the north, Jeb Stuart sat reading a letter of instructions from Lee:

> Headquarters, June 22, 1863
> Maj. Gen. J.E.B. Stuart,
>   Commanding Cavalry.
>   I have just received your note of 7:45 this morning to General Longstreet. I judge the efforts of the enemy yesterday were to arrest our progress and ascertain our whereabouts. Perhaps he is satisfied.

Do you know where he is and what he is doing? I fear he will steal a march on us, and get across the Potomac before we are aware. If you find that he is moving northward, and that two brigades can guard the Blue Ridge and take care of your rear, you can move with the other three into Maryland, and take position on General Ewell's right, place yourself in communication with him, guard his flank, keep him informed on the enemy's movements, and collect all the supplies you can for the use of the army. One column of General Ewell's army will probably move toward the Susquehanna by the Emmitsburg route; another by Chambersburg. Accounts from him last night state that there was no enemy west of Frederick. A cavalry force (about 100) guarded the Monocacy Bridge, which was barricaded. You will, of course, take charge of Jenkins' brigade, and give him necessary instructions. All supplies taken in Maryland must be by authorized staff officers for their respective departments—by no one else. They will be paid for, or receipts for the same given to the owners. I will send you a general order on this subject, which I wish you to see is strictly complied with.

On this same day Ewell received authorization from Lee to proceed with his entire Second Corps into Pennsylvania; the target—the capital city of Harrisburg. Longstreet was still in the Valley, preparing to move to the crossing of the Potomac. Hill's Third Corps was about to cross into Maryland.

Two days later, to ensure that Stuart understood his main duty in the coming operation, Lee further instructed him: "If General Hooker's army remains inactive, you can leave two brigades to watch him, and withdraw with the three others, but should he not appear to be moving northward, I think you had better withdraw this side of the mountains tomorrow night, cross at Shepherdstown next day, and move over to Frederickstown.

"You will, however, be able to judge whether you can pass around their army without hindrance, doing them all the damage you can, and cross the river east of the mountains. In either case, after crossing the river, you must move on and feel the right of Ewell's troops, collecting information, provisions, etc.

"Give instructions to the commander of the brigades left behind, to watch the flank and rear of the army, and (in the event of the enemy leaving their front) retire from the mountains west of the Shenandoah, leaving sufficient pickets to guard the passes, and bring everything clean along the Valley, closing upon the rear of the army.

"As regards the movements of the two brigades of the enemy moving toward Warrenton, the commander of the brigades to be left in the mountains must do what he can to counteract them, but I think the sooner you cross into Maryland, after tomorrow, the better.

"The movements of Ewell's corps are as stated in my former letter. Hill's first division will reach the Potomac today, and Longstreet will follow tomorrow.

"Be watchful and circumspect in all your movements."

In pondering Lee's words, Stuart was later to write:

In the exercise of the discretion vested in me by the commanding general, it was deemed practicable to move entirely in the enemy's rear, intercepting his communications with his base (Washington), and, inflicting damage upon his rear, to rejoin the army in Pennsylvania in time to participate in its actual conflicts.

Mindful of Lee's warning of the need for speed, Stuart ordered his troopers to take the road at one o'clock in the

morning of June 25 bound for Glasscock's Gap in the Bull
Run Mountain and thence on to Haymarket, where his
thousands of cavalrymen would turn north for the Potomac, Maryland, Pennsylvania, and the right flank of
Ewell's Second Corps.

But beyond Haymarket, Stuart's planned march hit a
snag when his troopers rode into Yankee infantry of Hancock's II Corps moving north along the route he had intended to take.

He sent off a report of Hancock's movement to Lee
before leading his troopers to the south and east.

It would be the last intelligence he would furnish his
commanding general for seven days.

On the morning of the 26th, having made the fateful
decision of continuing his march eastward instead of returning to the army by way of the Valley to the west, his
troopers rode out, first a little south of east, then north on
a route which would lead them between the city of Washington and the great bulk of Hooker's army moving north.

This would mean that thousands of bluecoats would be
swarming the countryside between them and the Army of
Northern Virginia for which they had been ordered to
provide the cavalry screen.

The late afternoon of that day would see Early's division
of Ewell's Second Corps capture the small town but important road center of Gettysburg, some nine miles north of
the Maryland-Pennsylvania line. This would put Stuart's
command almost eighty miles to the south.

On the same day Lee and Hill entered Chambersburg,
Pennsylvania, some thirty miles to the west of Gettysburg.

The commanding general had no news from Stuart or of
the position or movement of Hooker's host which he had
left back in Virginia.

He and his army were going it blind, and he was very
aware of the dangers this advance in the dark held for the
success of the operation.

June 27 saw Ewell's leading division capture Carlisle and the U.S. Army Cavalry barracks where he had once been stationed in the Old Army. The First and Third Corps were at Chambersburg with Lee, and he was still in the dark.

Where is Stuart?

That question was constantly before Lee who masked his concern with the appearance of quiet confidence.

Stuart that day was leading his cavalrymen northward at last to cross the Potomac at Rowser's Ford about fifteen miles northwest of Washington. The march was slow and tiresome due to the condition of both horses and men.

But on the 28th they were refreshed by the capture of a Federal wagon train, destroying many of the wagons in the attack but bringing 125 of them back to join the march north, now directed towards the town of Hanover. The wagons filled with booty when added to the prisoners taken, further slowed Stuart's progress.

That night the march resumed with an assault planned on the main line of the Baltimore and Ohio Railroad which Stuart's force would cross on their way to Hanover.

Although he had been out of contact with the army for three days, the flamboyant Jeb did not express any misgivings.

It was a different matter at headquarters where questions over his disappearance had gradually changed from concern to anxiety.

But the invasion must proceed.

Ewell would advance on Harrisburg.

Longstreet and Hill were prepared to follow.

June 29 was to witness large events.

But then fate intervened.

16

Spy Story

IN A DISTURBED STATE OF MIND, LEE SOUGHT HIS BED ON the night of June 28. But he did not rest long before he was aroused by Major John W. Fairfax who had been sent to him by Longstreet to report that the Army of the Potomac had crossed that river and was moving north on his trail.

How did he know?

Fairfax had the man with him who could vouch for the report.

Who was he?

He was a "scout" or spy, whom Longstreet had employed with good results.

Lee hesitated for he did not trust spies.

So he sent Fairfax away.

But later, driven by his need for information, he changed his mind and asked the man be sent to him.

It was a strange mid-night interview.

Illuminated by the lanterns in the headquarters tent sat Lee, calm and dignified, the gray-clad embodiment of the Southern Cause.

Facing him was Harrison, the spy, of mid-height, dark and wiry, his well cut civilian clothes stained and roughed up from the effects of his wild journey through the night. A Mississippian with a slight stoop, a beard and penetrating hazel eyes, he was in his way a symbol of the Southern Cause.

Still, no spy could be trusted.

It was so easy for one to be a double agent.

Yet Lee would hear him out.

It was quite a story.

Longstreet, who had employed Harrison on previous tasks, had called him to the headquarters of the First Corps before the army had marched away from Culpeper, and instructed him to go to Washington to gather whatever intelligence he could.

Harrison had made his way to the Federal capital where in the crowds, the hotel lobbies, and the saloons, he had picked up much gossip about the movements of Hooker's army.

But one item electrified the tired man who sat before the commanding general.

He had learned that Hooker's host had crossed over the fords of the Potomac headed north.

It was then he started for Frederick, Maryland, walking cross country by night, and mixing into the Northern columns of troops by day. He was right on target, for at Frederick he found two Union army corps with a third reported nearby.

Then, learning that the Army of Northern Virginia was

at Chambersburg, he had secured a horse and buggy from a Maryland sympathizer and had driven furiously to the north. On the way, he had seen Federal troops making for South Mountain beyond which ran Lee's line of communication with the South.

One other item of note: that very day Fighting Joe Hooker had been relieved of command of the Army of the Potomac, replaced by Lee's long time friend and brother Engineer officer in the Old Army, Major General George Gordon Meade.

What Harrison could not know was that Hooker, after a spat with the War Department, had submitted his resignation the day before. Immediately, a staff colonel had boarded a special train for Frederick from where he had arrived at Meade's V Corps headquarters at 3 A.M. on June 28 to offer him command of the Union Army.

At first Meade had refused "because others were better qualified," but on being told it was an order, he accepted, after which he was taken to Hooker's headquarters where the command change was effected much to Hooker's relief.

In taking over an army spread across the fields of Maryland, Meade was as blind to the future as his friend "Bob" Lee to the north. But he was just as tough, wiring the War Department: "I must move toward the Susquehanna, keeping Washington and Baltimore well covered, and if the enemy is checked in his attempt to cross the Susquehanna, or if he turns toward Baltimore, give him battle."

On the same evening Lee was talking to the spy Harrison, Meade had ordered the Army of the Potomac to be ready to march at daylight.

Lee was engaged in the same task of concentrating his forces for the battle which was to come.

Harrison had hardly left the headquarters tent before the orders were being drafted to send the couriers galloping through the night.

Ewell would halt his advance to the Susquehanna, on Harrisburg and beyond York, and instead march southward from Carlisle to Cashtown or Gettysburg.

Hill would put his Third corps on the road from Chambersburg to these two towns.

Longstreet would follow Hill with the First Corps the next day.

That afternoon he told some of his staff: "Tomorrow, gentlemen, we will not move to Harrisburg, as we expected, but will go over to Gettysburg and see what General Meade is after."

In commenting on the Federal change of command, he said: "General Meade will commit no blunder in my front, and if I make one he will make haste to take advantage of it."

That afternoon Heth's division of Hill's corps was closing Cashtown after a rainy, miserable march.

Still out of touch with the army, Stuart and his troopers were far to the south and east at a town called Westminister where at the railroad station they found ample supplies of food and forage that June 29 which again required time for distribution throughout the command. The following day they would be in Hanover, Pennsylvania, closing either on York, or Carlisle.

The invasion had stirred the North as nothing else in this bloody war. Governors of many of the states close to Pennsylvania were sending militia regiments to their stricken sister.

Washington itself was in a ferment. From Willard's Hotel to the sleaziest saloon in town almost any rumor would be believed.

The war wise city could sense that events then unfolding in the fields of Pennsylvania would certainly be critical to the direction of the war, even the destiny of the nation. What was it to be? Victory or defeat?

The next few days would decide.

17

To Get Some Shoes

E WELL'S SECOND CORPS WAS PREPARING TO START FOR Harrisburg and the Susquehanna when Lee's orders countermanding the march and ordering it to move southward where it would rejoin the other corps were received. Ewell ordered Early to leave York and rejoin him on the new line of march. Old Bald Head was unhappy with his orders but had no option but to comply.

So ended the most northerly penetration of the Army of Northern Virginia into enemy country during the war.

At Heidlersburg at nightfall on the thirtieth of June, Ewell received more orders from Lee directing him to move either to Cashtown or Gettysburg. They also fretted him because of their discretionary aspect. Under Jackson orders had been definite and exact.

At the same time, a note from A. P. Hill with the Third Corps at Cashtown reported that Union cavalry and perhaps other troops had been seen in Gettysburg.

After such a splendid advance march all the way from Virginia, the night of June 30 would see a puzzled and uncertain Ewell seek his rest.

There were few uncertainties in Hill's mind as he sent Heth's Division to lead the Third Corps advance on Cashtown and Gettysburg. Longstreet was to follow in his rear.

Johnston Pettigrew's brigade, leading the advance, moved out of Cashtown for Gettysburg, Pettigrew anxious to get into the town to find some shoes there for his barefooted men.

But he did not get his shoes.

He came back to Cashtown that afternoon to report to Heth that he had encountered Federal cavalry outposts in front of Gettysburg and some of his officers had heard the roll of drums indicating infantry was in the town.

Pettigrew, with no cavalry screen in his front to feel the enemy, brought his troops back to Cashtown.

Hill, arriving at Heth's headquarters shortly after, heard Pettigrew's tale but did not agree.

"The only force at Gettysburg is cavalry, probably a detachment of observation," he said. "I am just from General Lee, and the information he has from his scouts corroborates what I have received from mine—that is, the enemy are still at Middleburg (16 miles south of Gettysburg), and have not struck their tents."

"If there is no objection," Heth replied, "I will take my division tomorrow and go to Gettysburg and get those shoes."

Hill answered: "None in the world."

Stuart's troopers that day had captured Hanover then headed east and north en route to Carlisle, still with their

125 U.S. Quartermaster wagons, and still out of touch with Lee's army which had not heard a word from them for five days.

The cavalrymen spent the night of the thirtieth of June in the saddle, near the exhaustion point on their endless ride. It would be two more days before they saw the Army of Northern Virginia again.

Meade and his Army of the Potomac were having a frustrating time that last hot day of June, feeling to the north and west for the presence of their foe, the hair-trigger temper of their bearded, irascible commander, not soothed by the fog of war which surrounded him.

He had determined to move his army from Frederick northward to Harrisburg on a wide front to force Lee either to retreat or attack him before he could cross the Susquehanna, by so threatening his southern flank. At the same time, Meade would be protecting the great cities of Philadelphia, Baltimore and Washington.

As for a place to bring Lee to battle, he had decided a strong defensive position was afforded by the terrain along Pipe Creek, some 18 miles south and a little to the east of Gettysburg.

He had sent warning orders to his corps commanders to be ready to move there, while dispatching General John Buford and three brigades of cavalry to Gettysburg to screen the movement.

It was the sight of Buford's cavalry outposts which had turned back Pettigrew's shoe shopping expedition late that afternoon.

Impressed with the strength of the terrain south of Gettysburg, Buford sent couriers galloping back to Meade with the message that he would hold his present positions until the infantry and artillery could come up.

Immediately Meade ordered Major General John F.

Reynolds to advance on Gettysburg with his I Corps supported by Howard's XI Corps which was nearby, and by
Sickles' III Corps east of Emmitsburg.

Hard on the heels of the couriers carrying these orders,
more horsemen galloped off to the other corps commanders—Hancock, Sedgwick, Sykes, and Slocum, all bearing
the same message: Be prepared to close up for battle.

All roads led to Gettysburg.

Part IV

The die is cast.

—Plutarch

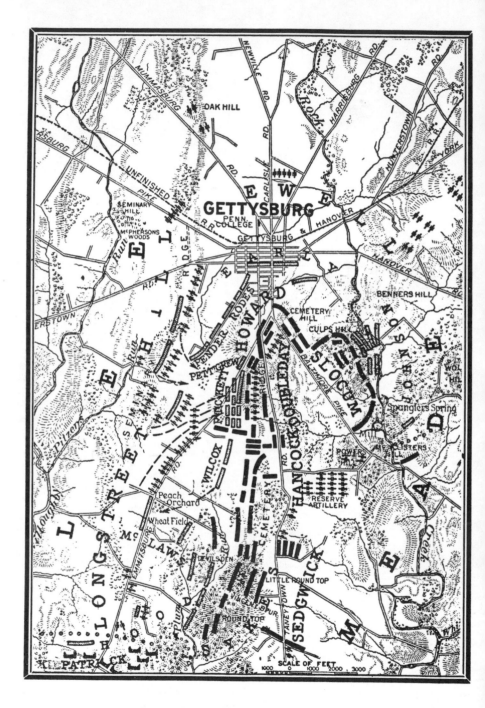

Battle of Gettysburg. Afternoon of July 3.

18

Reynolds Stakes a Claim

AT DAWN OF JULY 1, 1863, HARRY HETH'S INFANTRY WERE on the road from Cashtown to Gettysburg "to get some shoes."

It was a pleasant warm morning with intermittent rain showers sweeping over the advancing troops.

Nothing interfered with the march until about three miles west of Gettysburg when the leading units flushed Union cavalrymen who vanished into the misty morning. The long column then toiled up the slope of Herr Ridge which ran north and south on the western side of a small, slow flowing stream named Willoughby Run on the eastern side of which gently rose two heights destined to imprint their names on history, McPherson's and Seminary Ridges.

Up until this point the Confederates had met no resistance to their advance although there were signs of the enemy in abundance.

Riding up to the crest of Herr Ridge about eight o'clock, General Heth ordered his leading brigades to deploy on each side of the Cashtown Road and directed his artillery to shell the woodland on the opposite side of the run. But nothing happened so he sent his leading brigades forward to occupy the town.

Waiting for them were the unseen dismounted troopers of hard-eyed General Buford who was determined not to let them pass, stating: "My arrangements were made for entertaining him (Heth)."

First there came a spattering of fire directed at Heth's skirmish line as it came down the slope with gleaming bayonets, but this soon rose to a crescendo of noise as the whole line of rifles spit out their ire at the enemy.

Buford's artillery soon joined in adding to the din.

The Battle of Gettysburg had begun.

The Federal cavalrymen were proving to be tough customers, giving as good as they got from Heth's brigades which were being cut up.

But by nine o'clock, Buford could see from his observation post in the cupola atop the Lutheran Theological Seminary which gave the ridge its name, that his line was not going to hold on much longer.

At that moment he looked below him to see General Reynolds ride up from the south where the Army of the Potomac's left wing was advancing on Gettysburg.

"Can you hold on for a little while longer?" Reynolds asked.

"I reckon I can," the cavalryman responded.

Whereupon Reynolds sent a dispatch to Meade: "The

enemy is advancing in strong force. I will fight him inch by inch, and if driven into the town I will barricade the streets and hold him back as long as possible."

When Meade received this at his Taneytown headquarters, his face lit up.

"That is just like Reynolds," he said. "He will hold out to the bitter end."

When the leading brigde of Reynolds I Corps deployed from the road to join the action at Willoughby Run it did so with its fife and drum corps playing "The Campbells Are Coming." And come they did, rolling up the leading Confederate brigades and capturing a Confederate brigadier.

Heth himself, after shaking out his main battle line, held up his attack for two hours, mindful that Lee had not wanted to bring on a general engagement until all the Confederate corps were up.

After dispatching his note to Meade, Reynolds had galloped back to the head of the I Corps to lead it into action. He was doing this when he was shot dead from his horse.

Major General Abner Doubleday, of baseball fame, who had taken over I Corps when Reynolds had taken command of the army's left wing, was now the ranking Federal commander on the field.

The tempo of the fighting ebbed and flowed throughout the day. It was after 2 P.M. when Lee rode up to the battle lines as Heth was preparing another attack with General Pender's division in support.

Lee was still not certain of the size of the force that was facing Heth's men. Until he knew, he was loath to commit further troops to battle.

Astride Traveller he surveyed a confused scene.

Two of Heth's brigades had been badly hurt.

What damage had been done to Meade's forces?

He could not know.

Then from north of Gettysburg came the sound of firing. From his position behind Heth's lines, Lee could see through his glasses that some of the Federal units were altering their lines to face towards this new threat.

They began moving troops toward the north.

What could it be?

19

Hill Smashes Head On

As LEE PONDERED THE REASON FOR THE SHIFT OF DIREC-
tion of some of the Federal units facing the Third
Corps attack west of Gettysburg, the answer was not long
in coming.

From out of the woodland north of Gettysburg emerged
a long gray battle line, charging out to take the Federals of
the I Corps on their right flank and rear.

Now the shrill Rebel Yell could be heard as the troops
drove their attack home. But it was not going to be easy.
The I Corps veterans of what had been Reynolds' command, now Doubleday's, for he had turned over the direction of the field to Otis Howard, gave as good as they got
and soon they were driving Rodes' men of Ewell's Second
Corps.

Heth rode over to where Lee was watching the developing battle.

"Rodes is very heavily engaged," he said. "Had I not better attack?"

"No," Lee replied, "I am not prepared to bring on a general engagement today—Longstreet is not up."

But as they watched Rodes' division recoiling under the punishment being delivered by Doubleday's seasoned fighters, a new element appeared on the scene. Early's division of the Second Corps came in from the northeast to take them almost in reverse.

Lee, sensing a great chance for victory, sent Heth forward from Herr Ridge. He was followed by Pender's division of Hill's corps, and all of a sudden it was too much for the bluecoats. Beset from almost three sides, they retreated, fighting, through the town.

Lee closely followed his victorious troops, down the slopes of Herr Ridge and up the other side to the crest of Seminary Ridge. Dead and wounded were everywhere.

From his vantage point Lee could see Ewell's men battling their way through Gettysburg. About five thousand of Meade's soldiers were prisoners, about the same number dead.

South of the town he could also see a high hill which was the boldest feature of a group of hills. It had a fatal name—Cemetery Hill. The long ridge stretching away south of it to end in two turret-like peaks bore the fatal name, for this was known as Cemetery Ridge. The two twin peaks were known as Big and Little Round Tops.

Masses of defeated Federal troops were making their way to Cemetery Hill.

While he continued study of the ground, Lee ordered some of Hill's artillery to shell the hill where the bluecoats were seeking to rally.

As he looked through his glasses, he came to agreement

with his enemy, the hard-eyed cavalry general John Buford, who had reported to Meade, this was a very strong position.

But Lee saw as he watched the action that if Cemetery Hill could be seized, he would be in possession of the key to the whole field.

To that end, he turned to General A. P. Hill, who had been sick the entire day.

If, he told Hill, his divisions could take that high ground, the day's action would result in a complete victory for the South.

But Hill felt he had to decline.

His troops were fought out.

They could not do it.

Then, Lee concluded, it would be up to Ewell, so he sent a staff officer to the Second Corps commander to tell him he should "push those people" to capture Cemetery Hill without involving the whole army in a general engagement.

While Lee was issuing these orders, Longstreet rode up to study the Federal position through his glasses. They could both see that from Cemetery Hill the ground ran on eastward to two other heights which would become familiar to them as East Cemetery Hill and Culp's Hill.

With Culp's Hill trending somewhat to the south, the whole Federal position assumed the shape of a fish hook with Culp's Hill the barb, Cemetery Hill the curve of the bend, Cemetery Ridge the shank, and the two Round Tops the eyes through which might be passed the line.

The ground was strong indeed.

When Lee had finished with his staff aides and couriers, Longstreet put up his field glasses, and without waiting for invitation, gave his commanding general his appreciation of the situation and his advice on the future course of action.

"All we have to do," he said, "is to throw our army around by their left, and we shall interpose between the Federal army and Washington. We can get a strong position and wait, and if they fail to attack us we shall have everything in condition to move back tomorrow night in the direction of Washington, selecting beforehand a good position into which we can put our troops to receive battle the next day. Finding our object is Washington or that army, the Federals will be sure to attack us. When they attack, we shall beat them, as we proposed to do before we left Fredericksburg. The probabilities are that the fruits of our success will be great."

But because Meade's army was coming up to Gettysburg from the direction of Washington, Lee could not agree.

"If the enemy is there, we must attack him," Lee replied pointing at the foe.

Longstreet took Lee's answer with poor grace.

"If he is there, it will be because he is anxious that we should attack him—a good reason, in my judgment, for not doing so."

He then continued his argument but Lee said no more.

One of Ewell's aides rode up to inform Lee that Generals Rodes and Early believed they could take Cemetery Hill if they were supported on the right.

Lee replied: "Our people are not yet up, and I have no troops with which to occupy this higher ground."

It was about five o'clock.

At this time Major General Winfield Scott Hancock, commander of the II Corps galloped up to General Howard on Cemetery Hill. He had just come from Meade to take command of the field. Howard demurred but after the matter was adjusted, the Federal generals proceeded to strengthen their lines with troops they rallied from their repulse in front of Gettysburg.

Many of these men were from Howard's own XI Corps mixed with Doubleday's I Corps soldiers.

With firing quiet along the whole front, Lee prepared to ride to the left to confer with Ewell.

No attacks had been made on the Federal position on Cemetery Hill.

Why?

20

Ewell Hesitates in the Town

IT HAD BEEN A PUZZLING AND NOT ALTOGETHER SATISFACtory day for Ewell, that first day of July.

To begin with he had been unsettled with Lee's discretionary orders to move on either Cashtown or Gettysburg at his option. For the first time in the war it was becoming apparent that Old Bald Head really did not care for options. Under Jackson you always knew where you stood.

But here he was riding into Gettysburg to witness a victory in progress in which his own troops under Rodes and Early had played a major role.

Now that eternal problem of war—what to do next—would be up to him.

He looked to the south to observe the disordered fighting in the town from which the Federals were being driven.

Almost dead ahead of him loomed the eighty-foot height of Cemetery Hill, frowning down the main street of Gettysburg. Then to the east he could see two more heights, one, East Cemetery Hill at the same level, and then Culp's Hill rising one hundred feet higher.

To his soldier's eye it was apparent these hills dominated the entire field.

He was looking at the keys to the Battle of Gettysburg.

Some Federal troops seemed to be preparing to make a stand on Cemetery Hill, to which from the direction of Seminary Ridge streamed thousands of defeated bluecoats.

It was about four o'clock with some four hours of daylight remaining.

General John B. Gordon, whose brigade had spearpointed Early's troops to rescue Rodes threatened flank, rode up to Ewell's headquarters just north of Gettysburg for orders which would send him on and perhaps over Cemetery Hill and the bluecoats milling around its crest in the disorder of defeat.

But he received no orders.

Instead a mute Ewell sat his horse staring forward as if transfixed by the scene of battle.

Gordon waited out the precious minutes. But no words came.

Soon a staff officer from Edward Johnson's division rode up to inform Ewell that Johnson would arrive shortly and would be ready for immediate action.

Unable to contain himself longer, Gordon broke in to say he too was ready to attack and could assist Johnson in the capture of Cemetery Hill, if so ordered.

Ignoring Gordon and his offer, Ewell instructed

Johnson's aide that the division should advance to a forward position, then halt for further orders.

Whereupon he lifted his reigns and, with Gordon still by his side, rode into Gettysburg.

But they had not ridden far when Old Bald Head was struck by a minie ball.

Gordon cried out in alarm: "Are you hurt, Sir?"

A cool Ewell replied: "No, no, I'm not hurt. But suppose that ball had struck you: we would have had the trouble of carrying you off the field, sir. You see how much better fixed for a fight I am than you are. It don't hurt a bit to be shot in a wooden leg."

But still no order to advance on Cemetery Hill as the pair continued to ride into Gettysburg to reach the town square.

While his staff, many of whom had been with Stonewall, waited in disbelief at their general's inaction, one of them said: "Jackson is not here."

After they all had moved on to establish a temporary field headquarters on the edge of the town, General Isaac Trimble, who had left the Valley command to join Ewell as a voluntary aide, rode in to see his general.

"Well, General," he said, "we have had a grand success; are you not going to follow it up and push our advantage?"

Ewell replied that it was not General Lee's desire to bring on a general engagement until all his troops were up.

But the victory had changed all that, Trimble argued. The great chance offered the Confederates must be grasped.

Ewell's refusal to move angered his old friend who abruptly left to make his own survey of the ground to the front.

In a short time he was back to urge no time be lost in taking the hills south of Gettysburg.

"General," he said, pointing to Culp's Hill, "There is an eminence of commanding position, and not now occupied, as it ought to be, by us or by the enemy soon. I advise you to send a brigade and hold it if we are to remain here."

But after Ewell voiced further objections, Trimble lost his temper.

"Give me a brigade and I will engage to take that hill," he offered.

There was no reply.

"Give me a good regiment and I will do it!"

Still no reply.

Trimble, consumed with rage, walked away.

Shortly after, an aide he had sent to get Early's opinion as to where Johnson's division should be placed returned with "Old Jube's" counsel, that Johnson should move at once upon Culp's Hill.

But Ewell wanted to hear it first hand.

So a courier was sent to fetch Early to the field headquarters. Further action was delayed pending his arrival.

When Early finally appeared, he repeated his advice to take Culp's Hill and further suggested that Ewell and Hill attack Cemetery Hill from the north and the west.

Ewell then began to act. He ordered Johnson to move through Gettysburg preparatory to attack, and he sent an aide to General Lee to advise that he could assault Cemetery Hill if he had support from the west.

Before this aide could return, a member of Lee's staff rode up with the army commander's order to secure the heights if possible, and advising that Lee himself would visit Ewell shortly.

Ewell decided to have another look at the current situation, inviting Early to ride forward with him. At the southern edge of the town the two generals came under sharpshooters' fire. But although that did not bother Ewell, the activity of barking Union artillery from Cemetery Hill did, as did a report that a Federal column was making its way to Gettysburg by way of the York road.

So the pair turned back towards Ewell's headquarters, the Second Corps commander more set than ever to wait for Johnson's division to come up when it could be sent forward to capture Culp's Hill from where it would be easy to drive off the troublesome Yankee batteries. Early's arguments for an immediate attack were falling on deaf ears.

About this time Rodes joined them, so the three at Ewell's insistence, rode to the left to check the report of enemy on the York road. They did see skirmishers alongside the road but these were later to prove to be Confederates.

With the evening shadows darkening, Early rode off to his own command while Ewell and Rodes continued on back to the headquarters. Shortly Lee dismounted to join them with Ewell sending off a call for Early to come back.

All this time not a single organized attack had been mounted against the high ground to the south which loomed menacingly darker as the shadows enveloped Gettysburg.

But as the commanders of the Southern left wing sat with their chieftan, there was no talk of mounting an assault that night.

It already was too late.

So attention was turned to the following day.

It was soon apparent to Ewell that Lee intended to attack at the earliest possible moment.

He and Early and Rodes reported to the commanding general all the details they had on strength of their own units, what they knew of the enemy, ammunition supplies, and position of Johnson's division. When they had finished, Lee asked a question of Ewell.

"Can't you, with your corps, attack on this flank at daylight tomorrow?"

But Ewell was still pondering his response when Early jumped in.

Without a by-your-leave from anyone, he declared against any attack against Cemetery Hill the next day. By then he felt that an assault up the slopes against an enemy, who even now was probably fortifying his position was doomed to fail. Then he continued by calling attention to the Round Tops, now fading into the obscurity of the night. An attack on the right to capture these dominating knobs would, in his opinion, be more feasible and render the Federal position untenable

Ewell and Rodes were both in agreement.

After hearing them out, Lee asked: "Then perhaps I had better draw you around towards my right, as the line will be very long and thin if you remain here, and the enemy may come down and break through it?"

Early again usurped his corps commander's reply

No, he felt, the present position of the troops would make it very difficult for the Federals to come down off the heights and attack them.

Again Ewell and Rodes were in accord.

A dismayed Lee came to an understanding that he would attack on the right with Ewell demonstrating on the left. Both actions would be pressed to the utmost if successful. But he was not satisfied in his own mind. As if speaking to himself he said: "If I attack from my right, Longstreet will have to make the attack. Longstreet is a very good fighter when he gets in position and gets everything ready, but he is so slow."

When Lee mounted to ride back to Seminary Ridge after the conference, he was in a troubled state of mind. Here were the commanders of his left wing, who had participated in a great, if unexpected, victory during the morning and afternoon, all counseling defense and caution. He could not afford those two words.

As he rode back across that terrible field, he could not help contrast the conduct of his present commanders with that of Jackson that desperate day before Chancellorsville, who, upon riding into the defensive entrenchments of the Confederates facing the edge of the Wilderness, had up-ended everything with staccato orders changing defense to offense and leading to the South's greatest victory.

Well, Lee had no need to remind himself: Jackson was not here!

Upon returning to his Seminary Ridge headquarters, Lee had second thoughts about the attack plan he had approved on his visit to Ewell. He then sent a message to Ewell directing him to move and reinforce the right flank from where the main attack would be delivered in the morning. Everything else was cancelled.

But then another change.

Two of Ewell's staff officers had been on Culp's Hill and found no one there.

That changed everything.

Ewell mounted up to ride to Lee's headquarters under the light of a wan moon illuminating the horrid sights of the wide battlefield.

When Ewell told him he now thought Johnson could capture Cemetery Hill, an understanding Lee cancelled the previous orders, and directed Ewell to seize that high ground.

Longstreet was at the headquarters when it was decided to have Ewell regulate his movements according to the hour of the attack of the First corps.

There was no sign from him that he understood other-wise.

But for Ewell riding back to Gettysburg in the moonlight, there would be more unpleasant surprises before he sought his bed.

Upon arrival at his headquarters he sent an order to Johnson to occupy Culp's Hill. But Johnson had already tried. The returning officer reported that Johnson's advance party had found Federals on Culp's Hill, and in strength.

And if that were not enough, the same officer said that while he had been with Johnson, a Federal captured dispatch had been given him for Ewell. It was not encouraging to the general who read it in the light of a battle lantern at the end of a long day:

> Headquarters Fifth Corps
> Bonaughtown, July 2, 1863
>
> Major General Slocum:
> General: On the receipt of General Meade's note to you, of the 1st instant, I left Hanover at 7 P.M., and marched 9 miles to Bonaughtown, en route to Gettysburg. I shall resume my march at 4 A.M. Crawford's division had not reached Hanover at the hour I left there.
>
> Very respectfully, your
> obedient servant,
> George Sykes,
> Major-General, Commanding

Ewell shook his head. More Federal Army corps on their way to Gettysburg. Cemetery Hill in the hands of the Yankees.

But it was too late to do anything more.

The light of dawn was stealing across the Pennsylvania hills.

21

Meade Has No Choice

FOR GEORGE GORDON MEADE THE FIRST DAY OF JULY
brought jarring news from the battlefield.

Meade had spent a sleepless night before the battle
opened, dispatching orders to his widespread army corps
to concentrate on Gettysburg.

Reynolds would spearhead the advance, marching his I
Corps from Marsh Run to Gettysburg while Howard followed from Emmitsburg with the XI. Both of these corps
would be under Reynolds' control as commander of the
left wing.

The III Corps under Sickles would move up to Emmitsburg from Bridgeport.

Hancock would take his II Corps from Uniontown to Taneytown, present site of Meade's headquarters.

Slocum would bring up his XII Corps from Littlestown to Two Taverns and also take under his command Sykes' V Corps which would move up from Union Mills to Hanover. Kilpatrick's cavalry would move with these two units screening the right wing.

The remaining corps, Sedgwick's big VI, would remain at Manchester in reserve some thirty-four miles southeast of Gettysburg.

Certain Lee would not cross the Susquehanna, but uncertain as to the exact position of the major Confederate units, this pre-battle deployment of his corps preserved his flexibility of movement while at the same time covering Baltimore and Washington to the east and south.

Buford's reports of the Confederate advance on Gettysburg had done much to dissipate the fog of war which had enveloped Meade and his staff throughout an anxious night.

It was then Meade ordered Reynolds to take the I and XI Corps to hold on to Gettysburg while he ordered the rest of the Army of the Potomac to march swiftly to his support.

The report of Reynolds' death had been shattering to Meade who believed the I Corps leader, rather than himself, should have been given command of the Army of the Potomac.

Immediately Hancock had been ordered north to take over command of the field from Howard and Doubleday.

While Hancock was on his way, Meade learned of the collapse of the I and XI Corps battle line.

More couriers galloped off with urgent orders to speed the march of the converging corps.

Meade and his staff then prepared to move the headquarters north to the field of action where, from all reports, their effort to get enough troops on the line to repel the Rebels on the second day of the battle was going to be a very near thing.

It was late in the night when Meade surveyed the battle position.

Buford had been right.

It was very strong defensively.

But he had to have troops to man the long line.

Those troops were already coming, marching through the night to aid their beleaguered comrades imperiled by the long semi-circle of gray threatening to enclose them from the north and west. Most of them should be on the field by noon of the coming day.

Sedgwick's big VI Corps with more than thirty miles to cover would be the last to arrive. But his men should take their places on the battle line before the sun started to set.

So the methodical Meade could see it was going to be a very near thing indeed.

In Washington, Secretary of War Stanton and General-in-Chief of the Armies Halleck hung over the telegraph key waiting for the latest word from the great battle they knew had already commenced on the peaceful hills and fields of Pennsylvania.

There were two other men who thirsted for news from the front, where all their hopes and fears for the future would be hammered out in the blood and iron of combat.

In Richmond, President of the Confederacy Jefferson Davis,with his acute political sense, knew that all his aspirations for the future of his foundling nation depended on the success of Lee's gray-clad corps in Pennsylvania.

In the White House at Washington, President Abraham Lincoln hoped and prayed that this climactic battle would crush the rebellion.

Throughout the divided land people waited for the news as if they were almost afraid to hear it.

Part V

All delays are dangerous in war.
                    —John Dryden

22

Unwilling Warrior

Having had three hours sleep, Lee rode out in the very early morning darkness to his post of observation on Seminary Ridge. It was about 4 A.M.

Through his field glasses he swept the shadowy heights of Cemetery Hill, then south along Cemetery Ridge.

Cemetery Hill was still held by Federal troops but to the southward the crest of Cemetery Ridge seemed bare of soldiers.

Now was the time!

If an early attack could be launched against those positions, the remnants of Doubleday's I Corps and Howard's XI Corps would be assailed and destroyed before the rest of Meade's army could come up.

Time was vital.

And where were Longstreet's men?

He had stressed the need for early action and now his instrument was not to hand.

Frustrated by the inaction of Ewell on the previous day and now by the tardiness of Longstreet, Lee sent an aide to find out what was happening on Ewell's front on this crucial morning. If he could do little, Lee was ready to bring all his troops to the right.

An hour later Longstreet rode up with the head of his corps not far behind, but the line of march stretched out far to the west on the Chambersburg Road.

The tardy Longstreet was in a surly mood.

When his glasses showed the enemy still on Cemetery Hill, instead of speeding arrangements for the coming attack, he returned to his arguments of yesterday for a turning movement around the Federal left to force Meade into an attack on the Confederates in a defensive position of their choice.

Lee could not agree, holding that swift attack could result in a decisive victory.

A sick A. P. Hill rode up to join Lee and Longstreet in their talks.

It was now apparent there would be no early morning attack from Seminary Ridge.

On Cemetery Ridge, Meade who had spent a sleepless night positioning his troops, was now waiting anxiously the arrival of the rest of his army corps. These men had been on the road all night and the day before in answer to the alarm calls from Gettysburg.

As each brigade filed in to take their places in the battle line, his heart lifted slightly. But it was taking time and time was the one thing his old friend "Bob" Lee would deny to him if he could.

Asked by one of his generals how many men he expected to place on the field that day, he answered: "About 95,000—enough, I expect, for this business."

He paused before continuing: "Well, we may as well fight it out here as anywhere else."

By this time the ridge that had looked bare to Lee at dawn was beginning to fill up with blue-coated infantry and artillery.

Because Howard had dispatched a false report that the I Corps was fleeing from the field, Meade had replaced Doubleday with General John Newton, an action resented deeply by the I Corps veterans spread along the crests of Cemetery Hill and Culp's Hill beside their comrades of XI Corps.

On the far right, beyond Culp's Hill, Slocum's XII Corps were taking positions to ensure that there would be no envelopment of that exposed Federal flank.

Hancock's II Corps would extend southward from Cemetery Hill along Cemetery Ridge toward the Round Tops, with Sickles' III Corps holding the extreme Federal left.

Sykes' V Corps would be held in reserve near the Baltimore Pike, ready to move to any threatened part of the line.

Sedgwick's big VI Corps was forcing its march through killing heat and dust over boot tops.

At last Meade could feel that his Army of the Potomac was coming together.

Lee's army was coming together too. But at least one of its key commanders had not lost his sullen mood.

When General John B. Hood, riding at the head of his division of Longstreet's first Corps, arrived on Seminary Ridge, he spoke to Lee.

"The enemy is here," Lee said, "and if we do not whip him, he will whip us."

Hood gathered that Lee wanted his troops to deliver the assault as soon as possible.

But Longstreet overhearing the remark pulled Hood to one side.

"The general is a little nervous this morning," he said. "He wishes me to attack but I do not wish to do so without Pickett. I never like to go into battle with one boot off."

Pickett's division was far to the rear at this time and would not be available until late afternoon.

During these anxious hours Lee formed a new plan of attack in view of the building concentration of Federal troops on Cemetery Ridge. He had discovered there were good positions for his artillery at certain places on the Emmitsburg Road which ran northeast between the two ridges on into Gettysburg. If these were taken it would allow him to cover his oblique infantry advance on Cemetery Hill without too much risk of having the attack broken up by the Federal artillery.

So when General McLaws rode up at the head of what would be the leading division, Lee sent for him to explain the plan of attack.

"I wish you to place your division across this road," he said, showing him the place on the map and then across the valley before them. "I wish you to get there if possible without being seen by the enemy. Can you do it?"

"I know of nothing to prevent me," McLaws replied, "but I will take a party of skirmishers and go in advance and reconnoiter."

When Lee advised him that one of his staff was preparing to do just that, McLaws said he would go with him.

But Longstreet intervened, stating he did not wish McLaws to leave his division.

Then placing his finger on the map, he indicated a position.

"I wish your division placed so."

But Lee interposed.

"No, General, I wish it placed just opposite."

Confused by the conflict between his superiors, McLaws went back to his division.

Ignoring Longstreet's behavior, Lee called for Traveller

and rode off to Ewell's headquarters to see for himself the situation on the left, obviously expecting Longstreet to go ahead with the attack.

When he arrived at Ewell's headquarters about nine o'clock, he found the corps commander out making a survey of the lines with the staff officer Lee had sent to him early that morning.

In the interval Lee asked the fiery General Trimble to take him to a place where he could get a good look at the enemy position.

Trimble led him up into the cupola of the almshouse.

From that point Lee had a much closer view of the work the blue forces had done during the night and morning to strengthen their position.

"The enemy has the advantage of us in a short and inside line," he commented to his host, "and we are too much extended. We did not or could not pursue our advantage of yesterday and now the enemy is in a good position."

When Ewell returned, Lee instructed him to have the Second Corps conduct a demonstration when Longstreet attacked. If he found any advantageous openings, then he too should exploit them.

But there was still no sound of guns from Longstreet's lines.

Barely able to conceal his concern, Lee with his artillery expert, Armistead Long, turned back towards the center, observing the activities on Cemetery Ridge as they rode the lines.

Lee found all along the enemy lines that they were being made more powerful with each passing moment.

But still no sound of guns from the center of his line.

He could contain himself no longer.

"What can detain Longstreet! He ought to be in position now."

When he returned to Longstreet's headquarters he

found little had been done in preparation for the coming
attack.

Lee then had to directly order him to start the operation.
Even then he found further reason for delay.

But at long last the columns started moving.

It was midday.

23

Sulkiness or Disobedience?

THE BALEFUL SPIRIT OF CONTENTION WHICH HAD ENWRAP-
ped Longstreet since he first rode up to join Lee on
Seminary Ridge now took a perverse turn.

If the commanding general did not want his advice, so
be it.

Where before he had argued his points, he would now
ensure that every detail of Lee's orders would be obeyed to
the letter—obeyed literally even though changing conditions of battle and plain common sense might dictate
otherwise.

It was a mood which would prove deadly to thousands

of the brave gray-coated soldiers with which he marched forward under the blistering July sun.

Responsibility for the march he placed on Lee's young staff officer who had made an early morning reconnaissance on the right, and who had explained the ground to Longstreet's leading division commander, General McLaws.

When the road on which they were marching came to a point where the troops would be exposed to enemy observation, the staff officer suggested to Longstreet a by-pass route which offered concealment. But Longstreet would have none of it. They would follow the road, and he ordered Hood's division to pass McLaws and take the lead.

Hood challenged Longstreet after the war:

"This movement was accomplished by throwing out an advanced force to tear down fences and clear the way. The instructions I received were to place my division across the Emmitsburg Road, form line of battle, and attack. Before reaching this road, however, I had sent forward some of my picked Texas scouts to ascertain the position of the enemy's extreme left flank. They soon reported to me that it rested upon Round Top Mountain; that the country was open and that I could march through an open woodland pasture around Round Top and assault the enemy in flank and rear; and that their wagon trains were parked in rear of their line, and were badly exposed to our attack in that direction. As soon as I arrived upon the Emmitsburg Road I placed one or two batteries in position and opened fire. A reply from the enemy's guns soon developed his lines. His left rested on or near Round Top, with the line bending back and again forward, forming, as it were, a concave line as approached by the Emmitsburg Road. A considerable body of troops was posted in front of their main line, between the Emmitsburg Road and Round top Mountain.

This force was in line of battle upon an eminence near a peach orchard.

"I found, that in making the attack according to orders, viz: up the Emmitsburg Road, I should have first to encounter and drive off this advanced line of battle; secondly, at the base and along the slope of the mountain, to confront immense boulders of stone, so massed together as to form narrow openings, which would break our ranks and cause the men to scatter whilst climbing up the rocky precipice. I found, moreover, that my division would be exposed to a heavy fire from the main line of the enemy, in position on the crest of the high range, of which Round Top was the extreme left, and, by reason of the concavity of the enemy's main line, that we would be subject to a destructive fire in flank and rear, as well as in front; and deemed it almost an impossibility to clamber along the boulders up this steep and rugged mountain, and, under this number of cross fires, put the enemy to flight. I knew that if the feat was accomplished it must be at a most fearful sacrifice of as brave and gallant soldiers as ever engaged in battle.

"The reconnaissance by my Texas scouts and the development of the Federal lines were effected in a very short space of time; in truth, shorter than I have taken to recall and jot down these facts, although the scenes and events of that day are as clear to my mind as if the great battle had been fought yesterday. I was in possession of these important facts so shortly after reaching the Emmitsburg Road that I considered it my duty to report to you at once my opinion, that it was unwise to attack up the Emmitsburg Road, as ordered, and to urge that you allow me to turn Round Top and attack the enemy in flank and rear. Accordingly, I dispatched a staff officer bearing to you my request to be allowed to make the proposed movement on account of the above-stated reasons. Your reply was quickly received: 'Gen'l Lee's orders are to attack up the Emmitsburg Road.' I sent another officer to say that I feared nothing could be accomplished by such an attack, and renewed my request to turn Round Top. Again your answer was: 'Gen'l Lee's orders are to attack up the Emmitsburg Road.' During this interim I had continued the use of the batteries upon the enemy, and had become more and more convinced that the Federal line extended to Round Top, and that I could not reasonably hope to accomplish much by the attack as ordered. In fact it seemed to me the enemy occupied a position by nature so strong—I may say impregnable—that, independently of their flank-fire, they could easily repel our attack by merely throwing and rolling stones down the mountain side as we approached.

"A third time I dispatched one of my staff to explain fully in regard to the situation, and to suggest that you had better come and look for yourself. I selected, in this instance, my adjutant general, Colonel Harry Sellers, whom you know to be not only an officer of great courage, but also of marked ability. Colonel Sellers returned with the same message: 'Gen'l Lee's orders are to attack up the Emmitsburg Road.' Almost simultaneously, Col. Fairfax, of your staff, rode up and repeated the above orders.

"After this urgent protest against entering into battle at Gettysburg according to instructions—which protest is the first and only one I ever made during my entire military career—I ordered my line to advance and make the assault.

"As my troops were moving forward, you rode up in person; a brief conversation passed between us, during which I again expressed the fears above mentioned, and regret at not being allowed to attack in flank around Round Top. You answered to this effect: 'We must obey the orders of General Lee.' I then rode forward with my line under a heavy fire. In about twenty minutes after reaching the Peach Orchard I was severely wounded in the arm, and borne from the field.

"With this wound terminated my participation in this great battle. As I was borne off on a litter to the rear, I could but experience deep distress of mind and heart at the thought of the inevitable fate of my brave fellow soldiers, who formed one of the grandest divisions of that world-renowned army; and I shall ever believe that had I been permitted to turn Round Top Mountain, we would not only have gained that position, but have been able finally to rout the enemy."

So far had the black resentment of Longstreet corroded his mind and spirit.

All of this was happening about 3:30 P.M. to an attack that had been supposed to have jumped off in the early morning hours.

Just to the north on Hood's left, General McLaws was getting the same treatment from Longstreet.

When asked by Old Pete why he had not attacked, he replied that the Federals were in his front around the Peach Orchard in great strength both in infantry and artillery.

Longstreet snorted. There was nothing there but a regiment and a battery.

McLaws then requested an artillery preparation against the Union guns to assure the success of the division's attack. But Longstreet would not hear of it.

When requested to come forward and see for himself, he refused, harshly telling him that he was in the position assigned by Lee, for the attack ordered by Lee, and he and his troops must go forward in accordance with Lee's orders forthwith.

Across the valley, Meade was having his own command problems.

He had posted the III Corps under General Daniel Sickles whom he heartily disliked, to hold the southern flank of the Cemetery Ridge line to include the two Round Tops.

But Sickles had not liked the ground assigned to him because as the ridge ran south from Cemetery Hill it lost elevation, so much so, he had selected another battle position and disregarded the Round Tops altogether.

Consequently the uneasy veterans of the III Corps found themselves thrown forward about a mile in front of the army's main battle line, some units strung along the Emmitsburg Road in a northeasterly direction while others would face southwest occupying such terrain features as the Peach Orchard, the Wheat Field, and the Devil's Den—all names that would ring ominously in any litany of American military history.

With this sharp bend in his forward line, Sickles had created a ready-made salient open to Confederate attack from two sides.

Late in the afternoon when the Rebel attack was getting underway, Meade rode out to the left to see for himself. He was angered and appalled.

"General," he said, "you are too far out."

Sickles replied he would withdraw.

His offer was punctuated with shell bursts.

"I wish to God you could," Meade shouted, "but those people will not permit it."

The interchange was prelude to some of the bloodiest fighting of the entire war.

On Seminary Ridge just after Longstreet's corps marched off to its long delayed attack, Jeb Stuart rode up to confront his long suffering general.

It was a most painful reunion but Lee could not remain angry with his favorite cavalryman for very long.

In the end he asked him: "Help me fight these people."

For late as it was in the day, the great events of that scarlet afternoon were just beginning.

24

On the Round Tops

W HEN HOOD SENT HIS DIVISION FORWARD THAT SWEL-
tering afternoon of July 2, his right flank brigade
under General Law found itself being pushed by the terrain towards the slopes of the Big Round Top in spite of the
repeated orders to attack up the Emmitsburg Road.

Colonel William C. Oates, commanding the 15th Alabama, the extreme right flank regiment stated:

"General Law rode up to me as we were advancing, and
informed me that I was then on the extreme right of our
line and for me to hug the base of Great Round Top and go
up the valley between the two mountains until I found the
left of the Union line, to turn it and do all the damage I
could, and that Lieutenant-Colonel Bulger would be instructed to keep the 47th closed to my regiment, and if

separated from the brigade he should act under my orders.

"Just after we crossed Plum Run we received the first fire from the enemy's infantry. It was Stoughton's Second Regiment United States sharpshooters, posted behind a fence at or near the southern foot of Great Round Top. They reached that position as we advanced through the old field. No other troops were there nor on that mountain at that time. I did not halt at the first fire, but looked to the rear for the 48th Alabama, and saw it going, under General Law's order, across the rear of our line to the left, it was said, to reenforce the Texas brigade, which was hotly engaged. That left no one in my rear or on my right to meet this foe. They were in the woods and I did not know the number of them.

"I received the second fire. Lieutenant-Colonel Feagin and one or two of the men fell. I knew it would not do to go on and leave that force, I knew not how strong, in our rear with no troops of ours to take care of them; so I gave the command to change direction to the right. The seven companies of the 47th swung around with the 15th and kept in line with it. The other three companies of that regiment were sent forward as skirmishers before the advance began. The sharpshooters retreated up the south front of the mountain, pursued by my command.

"In places the men had to climb up, catching to the rocks and bushes and crawling over the boulders in the face of the fire of the enemy, who kept retreating, taking shelter and firing down on us from behind the rocks and crags which covered the side of the mountain thicker than grave-stones in a city cemetery. Fortunately they usually over-shot us. We could see our foe only as they dodged back from one boulder to another, hence our fire was scattering. As we advanced up the mountain they ceased firing about half-way up, divided, and a battalion went around the mountain on each side. Those who went up to the right fired a few shots at my flank. To meet this I deployed Company A, and moved it by the left flank to protect my right, and continued my rugged ascent until we reached the top.

"Some of my men fainted from heat, exhaustion, and thirst. I halted and let them lie down and rest a few minutes. . . . I saw Gettysburg through the foliage of the trees. Saw the smoke and heard the roar of battle which was then raging at the Devil's Den, in the peach orchard, up the Emmitsburg road, and on the west and south of the Little Round Top. I saw from the highest point of rocks that we were then on the most commanding elevation in that neighborhood. I knew that my men were too much exhausted to make a good fight without a few minutes rest. . . .

"When we formed line of battle before the advance began, a detail was made of two men from each of the eleven companies of my regiment to take all the canteens to a well about one hundred yards in our rear and fill them with cool water before we went into fight. Before this detail could fill the canteens the advance was ordered. . . . the water detail followed with the canteens of water, but when they got into the woods they missed us, walked right into the Yankee lines, and were captured, canteens and all. My men in the ranks, in the intense heat, suffered greatly for water. The loss of these 22 men and lack of the water contributed largely to our failure to take Little Round Top a few minutes later. About five minutes after I halted, Captain Terrell, assistant adjutant-general to General Law, rode up by the only pathway on the southeast side of the mountain and inquired why I had halted. I told him. He then informed me that General Hood was wounded, Law was in command of the division, and sent me his compliments, said for me to press on, turn the Union left, and capture Little Round Top, if possible, and to lose no time.

"I then called his attention to my position. A precipice

on the east and north, right at my feet; a very steep, stony, and wooded mountain-side on the west. The only approach to it by our enemy, a long wooded slope on the northwest. Within half an hour I could convert it into a Gibraltar that I could hold against ten times the number of men that I had, hence in my judgment it should be held and occupied by artillery as soon as possible, as it was higher than the other mountain and would command the entire field. Terrell replied that probably I was right, but that he had no authority to change or originate orders.   .
He then repeated that General Law had sent him to tell me to lose no time, but to press forward and drive everything before me as far as possible.

"Just as the 47th companies were being driven back, I ordered my regiment to change direction to the left, swing around, and drive the Federals from the ledge of rocks, for the purpose of enfilading their line, relieving the 47th— gain the enemy's rear, and drive him from the hill. My men obeyed and advanced about half way to the enemy's position, but the fire was so destructive that my line wavered like a man trying to walk against a strong wind, and then slowly, doggedly, gave back a little; then with no one upon the left or right of me, my regiment exposed, while the enemy was still under cover, to stand there and die was sheer folly; either to retreat or advance became a necessity. . . .

"I again ordered the advance, and knowing the officers and men of that gallant old regiment, I felt sure that they would follow their commander anywhere in the line of duty. I passed through the line waving my sword, shouting, 'Forward, men, to the ledge!' and was promptly followed by the command in splendid style. We drove the Federals from their strong defensive position; five times they rallied and charged us, twice coming so near that some of my men had to use the bayonet, but in vain was their effort. It was our time now to deal death and destruction to a gallant foe, and the account was speedily settled. I led this charge and sprang upon the ledge of rock, using my pistol within musket length, when the rush of my men drove the Maine men from the ledge along the line. . . . At this angle and to the southwest of it is where I lost the greatest number of my men. The 20th Maine was driven back from this ledge, but not farther than to the next ledge on the mountain-side. . . .

"I, with my regiment, made a rush forward from the ledge. About forty steps up the slope there is a large boulder about midway the Spur. The Maine regiment charged my line, coming right up in a hand-to-hand encounter. My regimental colors were just a step or two to the right of that boulder, and I was within ten feet. A Maine man reached to grasp the staff of the colors when Ensign Archibald stepped back and Sergeant Pat O'Connor stove his bayonet through the head of the Yankee, who fell dead. . . .

"There never were harder fighters than the 20th Maine men and their gallant Colonel. His skill and persistency and the great bravery of his men saved Little Round Top and the Army of the Potomac from defeat. Great events sometimes turn on comparatively small affairs. My position rapidly became untenable. The Federal infantry were reported to be coming down on my right and certainly were closing in on my rear, while some dismounted cavalry were closing the only avenue of escape on my left rear. I sent my sergeant-major with a request to Colonel Bowles, of the 4th Alabama, the next in line to the left, to come to my relief. He returned within a minute and reported that none of our troops were in sight, the enemy to be between us and the 4th Alabama, and swarming the woods south of Little Round Top. The lamented Captain Park, who was afterwards killed at Knoxville, and Captain

Hill, killed near Richmond in 1864, came and informed me that the enemy were closing in on our rear. I sent Park to ascertain their number. He soon returned, and reported that two regiments were coming up behind us, and just then I saw them halt behind a fence, some two hundred yards distant, from which they opened fire on us. These, I have since learned from him, were the battalions of Stoughton's sharp-shooters, each of which carried a flag, hence the impression that there were two regiments. They had been lost in the woods, but, guided by the firing, came up in our rear. At Balaklava, Captain Nolan's Six Hundred had cannon to the right of them, cannon to the left of them, cannon in front of them, which volleyed and thundered. But at this moment the 15th Alabama had infantry in front of them, to the right of them, dismounted cavalry to the left of them, and infantry in the rear of them. With a withering and deadly fire pouring in upon us from every direction, it seemed that the regiment was doomed to destruction. While one man was shot in the face, his right-hand or left-hand comrade was shot in the side or back. Some were struck simultaneously with two or three balls from different directions. Captains Hill and Park suggested that I should order a retreat; but this seemed impracticable. My dead and wounded were then nearly as great in number as those still on duty. They literally covered the ground. The blood stood in puddles in some places on the rocks; the ground was soaked with the blood of as brave men as ever fell on the red field of battle.

"I still hoped for reenforcements or for the tide of success to turn my way. It seemed impossible to retreat and I therefore replied to my captains, "Return to your companies; we will sell out as dearly as possible."

Hill made no reply, but Park smiled pleasantly, gave me the military salute, and said "All right, sir."

"On reflection a few moments later I saw no hope of

success and did order a retreat, but did not undertake to retire in order. I sent Sergeant-Major Norris and had the officers and men advised the best I could that when the signal was given that we would not try to retreat in order, but every one should run in the direction from whence we came, and halt on the top of the Big Round Top Mountain. I found the undertaking to capture Little Round Top too great for my regiment unsupported. I waited until the next charge of the 20th Maine was repulsed, as it would give my men a better chance to get out unhurt, and then ordered the retreat. . . .

"When the signal was given we ran like a herd of wild cattle, right through the line of dismounted cavalrymen. Some of the men as they ran through seized three of the cavalrymen by the collar and carried them out prisoners."

So ended the Southern thrust at Meade's left flank. That Hood's men were thrown off the Round tops at all can be credited to General G. K. Warren, Meade's chief engineer officer who had been sent by Meade to check the left flank of the line.

He arrived on Little Round Top to find none of Sickles' men there, about the time Longstreet's divisions went smashing in to the exposed positions of the III Corps in the Peach Orchard and along the Emmitsburg Road.

Porter Farley of the 140th New York Volunteers, Sykes V Corps, moving up from reserve, to aid Sickles, was there:

"The leading regiments of our brigade were just passing over that slightly elevated ground north of Little Round Top when down its slopes on our left, accompanied by a single mounted officer and an orderly, rode General G. K. Warren, our former brigade commander, then acting as General Meade's chief engineer. Warren came straight toward the head of the regiment, where I was riding with the colonel. He called out to O'Rorke, beginning to speak while still some eight or ten rods from us, that he wanted

us to come up there, that the enemy were advancing
unopposed up the opposite side of the hill, down which
he had just come, and he wanted our regiment to meet
them. He was evidently greatly excited and spoke in his
usual impulsive style.

"O'Rorke answered, 'General Weed is ahead and expects me to follow him.'

" 'Never mind that,' said Warren, 'bring your regiment
up here and I will take the responsibility.'

"It was a perplexing situation, but without hesitating
O'Rorke turned to the left and followed the officer who
had been riding with Warren, while Warren himself rode
rapidly down the stony hill, whether in the direction from
which we had just come or to overtake the rest of our
brigade I cannot say, but evidently to find and order up
more troops. . . .

"We turned off the road to our left and rushed along the
wooded, rocky, eastern slope of Little Round Top, ascend-
ing it while at the same time moving toward its southern
extremity. It was just here that some of the guns of
Hazlett's battery came rapidly up and plunged directly
through our ranks, the horses being urged to frantic
efforts by the whips of their drivers and the cannoniers
assisting at the wheels, so great was the effort necessary to
drag the guns and caissons up the ragged hillside.

"As we reached the crest a never to be forgotten scene
burst upon us. A great basin lay before us full of smoke
and fire, and literally swarming with riderless horses and
fighting, fleeing and pursuing men. The air was saturated
with the sulphurous fumes of battle and was ringing with
the shouts and groans of the combatants. The wild cries of
charging lines, the rattle of musketry, the booming of
artillery and the shrieks of the wounded were the or-
chestral accompaniments of a scene like very hell itself—as
terrific as the warring of Milton's fiends in Pandemonium.

The whole of Sickles' corps, and many other troops which had been sent to its support in that ill-chosen hollow, were being slaughtered and driven before the impetuous advance of Longstreet. But fascinating as was this terrible scene we had no time to spend upon it. Bloody work was ready for us at our very feet.

"Round Top, a conical hill several hundred feet in height, lay just to the south of us, and was separated from Little Round Top, on whose crest we were now moving, by a broad ravine leading down into the basin where the great fight was raging. Right up this ravine, which offered the easiest place of ascent, a Rebel force, outflanking all our troops in the plain below, was advancing at the very moment when we reached the crest of the hill. Vincent's brigade of the First Division of our corps had come up through the woods on the left and were just getting into position, and the right of their line had opened fire in the hollow on our left when the head of our regiment came over the hills. As soon as we reached the crest bullets came flying in among us. We were moving with the right in front and not a musket was loaded, a fact which Warren, of course, knew nothing about when he rushed us up there. The enemy were coming from our right and to face them would bring our file closers in front. The order, 'On the right, by file into line,' would have brought us into proper position; but there was no time to execute it, not even time to allow the natural impulse which manifested itself on the part of the men to halt and load the instant we received the enemy's fire.

"O'Rorke did not hesitate a moment. 'Dismount,' said he to me, for the ground before us was too rough to ride over. We sprung from our horses and gave them to the sergeant major. O'Rorke shouted, 'Down this way, boys,' and following him we rushed down the rocky slope with all the same moral effect upon the Rebels, who saw us coming, as if our bayonets had been fixed and we ready to charge upon them. Coming abreast of Vincent's brigade, and taking advantage of such shelter as the huge rocks lying about there afforded, the men loaded and fired, and in less time than it takes to write it, the onslaught of the Rebels was fairly checked. In a few minutes the woods in front of us were cleared except for the dead and wounded. Such of the Rebels as had approached so near as to make escape almost impossible dropped their guns, threw up their hands, and upon a slight slackening of our fire rushed in upon us and gave themselves up as prisoners, while those not so near took advantage of the chance left them and retreated in disorder."

Theodore Gerrish, a private in the 20th Maine, picked up the action: "At daylight, on the morning of July 2d, we resumed our march, and in a few hours halted within supporting distance of the left flank of our army, about a mile to the right of Little Round Top. The long forenoon passed away, and to our surprise the enemy made no attack. This was very fortunate for our army, as it enabled our men to strengthen our lines of fortifications, and also to obtain a little rest, of which they were in great need. The Rebels were also engaged in throwing up rude lines of defenses, hurrying up reinforcements, and in discussing the line of action they should pursue. . . .

"The hour of noon passed, and the sun had measured nearly one-half the distance across the western sky before the assault was made. Then, as suddenly as a bolt of fire flies from the storm cloud, a hundred pieces of Rebel artillery opened upon our left flank, and under the thick canopy of screaming, hissing, bursting shells, Longstreet's corps was hurled upon the troops of General Sickles. Instantly our commanders discerned the intention of General Lee. It was to turn and crush our left flank, as he had crushed our right at Chancellorsville. It was a terrible onslaught. The brave sons of the south never displayed more gallant courage than on that fatal afternoon of July 2. But brave Dan Sickles and the old Third Corps were equal to the emergency, and stood as immovable against the surging tides as blocks of granite. But a new and appalling danger suddenly threatened the Union Army. Little Round Top was the key to the entire position. Rebel batteries planted on that rocky bluff could shell any portion of our line at their pleasure. For some reason Sickles had not placed any infantry upon this important position. A few batteries were scattered along its ragged side, but they had no infantry support.

"Lee saw at a glance that Little Round Top was the prize for which the two armies were contending, and with skillful audacity he determined to wrest it from his opponent. While the terrible charge was being made upon the line of General Sickles, Longstreet threw out a whole division by extending his line to his right, for the purpose of seizing the coveted prize. The danger was at once seen by our officer, and our brigade was ordered forward, to hold the hill against the assault of the enemy. In a moment all was excitement. Every soldier seemed to understand the situation, and to be inspired by its danger. 'Fall in! Fall in! By the right flank! Double-quick! March!' and away we went, under the terrible artillery fire. It was a moment of thrilling interest. Shells were exploding on every side. Sickles' corps was enveloped in sheets of flame, and looked like a vast windrow of fire. But so intense was the excitement that we hardly noticed these surroundings. Up the steep hillside we ran, and reached the crest. 'On the right by file into line,' was the command, and our regiment had assumed the position to which it had been assigned. We were on the left of our brigade, and consequently on the extreme left of all our line of battle. The ground sloped to our front and left, and was sparsely covered with a growth

of oak trees, which were too small to afford us any protection. Shells were crashing through the air above our
heads, making so much noise that we could hardly hear
the commands of our officers; the air was filled with fragments of exploding shells and splinters torn from mangled
trees; but our men appeared to be as cool and deliberate in
their movements as if they had been forming a line upon
the parade ground in camp.

"Our regiment mustered about three hundred and fifty
men. Company B, from Piscataquis County, commanded
by the gallant Captain Morrill, was ordered to deploy in
our front as skirmishers. They boldly advanced down the
slope and disappeared from our view. Ten minutes have
passed since we formed the line; the skirmishers must
have advanced some thirty or forty rods through the rocks
and trees, but we have seen no indications of the enemy;
'But look! Look! Look!' exclaimed half a hundred men in
our regiment at the same moment; and no wonder, for
right in our front, between us and our skirmishers, whom
they have probably captured, we see the lines of the enemy. They have paid no attention to the rest of the brigade
stationed on our right, but they are rushing on, determined to turn and crush the left of our line. Colonel
Chamberlain with rare sagacity understood the movement
they were making, and bent back the left flank of our
regiment until the line formed almost a right angle with
the colors at the point, all these movements requiring a
much less space of time than it requires for me to write of
them.

"How can I describe the scenes that followed? Imagine if
you can, nine small companies of infantry, numbering
perhaps three hundred men, in the form of a right angle,
on the extreme flank of an army of eighty thousand men,
put there to hold the key of the entire position against a
force at least ten times their number, and who are desper-

ately determined to succeed in the mission upon which they came. Stand firm, ye boys from Maine, for not once in a century are men permitted to bear such responsibilities for freedom and justice, for God and humanity, as are now placed upon you.

"The conflict opens. I know not who gave the first fire, or which line received the first lead. I only know that the carnage began. Our regiment was mantled in fire and smoke. I wish that I could picture with my pen the awful details of that hour—how rapidly the cartridges were torn from the boxes and stuffed in the smoking muzzles of the guns; how the steel rammers clashed and clanged in the heated barrels; how the men's hands and faces grew grim and black with burning powder; how our little line, baptized with fire, reeled to and fro as it advanced or was pressed back; how our officers bravely encouraged the men to hold on and recklessly exposed themselves to the enemy's fire—a terrible medley of cries, shouts, cheers, groans, prayers, curses, bursting shells, whizzing rifle bullets and clanging steel. And if that was all, my heart would not be so sad and heavy as I write. But the enemy was pouring a terrible fire upon us, his superior forces giving him a great advantage. Ten to one are fearful odds where men are contending for so great a prize. The air seemed to be alive with lead. The lines at times were so near each other that the hostile gun barrels almost touched. As the contest continued, the Rebels grew desperate that so insignificant a force should so long hold them in check. At one time there was a brief lull in the carnage, and our shattered line was closed up, but soon the contest raged again with renewed fierceness. The Rebels had been reinforced, and were now determined to sweep our regiment from the crest of Little Round Top.

"Many of our companies have suffered fearfully. . . . But there is no relief, and the carnage goes on. Our line is pressed back so far that our dead are within the lines of the enemy. The pressure made by the superior weight of the enemy's line is severely felt. Our ammunition is nearly all gone, and we are using the cartridges from the boxes of our wounded comrades. A critical moment has arrived, and we can remain as we are no longer; we must advance or retreat. It must not be the latter, but how can it be the former? Colonel Chamberlain understands how it can be done. The order is given 'Fix bayonets!' and the steel shanks of the bayonets rattle upon the rifle barrels. 'Charge bayonets, charge!' Every man understood in a moment that the movement was our only salvation, but there is a limit to human endurance, and I do not dishonor those brave men when I write that for a brief moment the order was not obeyed, and the little line seemed to quail under the fearful fire that was being poured upon it. O for some man reckless of life, and all else save his country's honor and safety, who would rush far out to the front, lead the way, and inspire the hearts of his exhausted comrades!

"In that moment of supreme need the want was supplied. Lieutenant H. S. Melcher, an officer who had worked his way up from the ranks, and was then in command of Company F, at the time the color company, saw the situation, and did not hesitate, and for his gallant act deserves as much as any other man the honor of the victory on Round top. With a cheer, and a flash of his sword that sent an inspiration along the line, full ten paces to the front he sprang—ten paces—more than half the distance between the hostile lines. 'Come on! Come on! Come on, boys!' he shouts. The color sergeant and the brave color guard follow, and with one wild yell of anguish wrung from its tortured heart, the regiment charged.

"The Rebels were confounded at the movement. We struck them with a fearful shock. They recoil, stagger, break and run, and like avenging demons our men pursue. The Rebels rush toward a stone wall, but, to our mutual surprise, two scores of rifle barrels gleam over the rocks, and a murderous volley was poured in upon them at close quarters. A band of men leap over the wall and capture at least a hundred prisoners. Piscataquis has been heard from, and as usual it was a good report. This unlooked-for reinforcement was Company B, who we supposed were all captured.

"Our colonel's commands were simply to hold the hill, and we did not follow the retreating Rebels but a short distance. After dark an order came to advance and capture a hill in our front. Through the trees, among the rocks, up the steep hillside, we made our way, captured the position, and also a number of prisoners."

With Little Round Top in Federal hands, the action began working its way northward to add three more names to the sinister history of the Battle of Gettysburg: Devil's Den, the Peach Orchard and the Wheat Field.

25

Devil's Den, Peach Orchard, Wheat Field

WHILE HOOD'S RIGHT BRIGADE UNDER LAW WAS BEING forced by the tide of battle up the craggy slopes of Little Round Top, a second brigade commanded by Brigadier General George T. Anderson, was advancing through the weird, almost spectral maze of immense rocks scattered every which way amongst ugly, scraggly trees at the foot of the rise below the Peach Orchard where stood the embattled artillery and infantry of Sickles' III corps.

At the best of times it was a forbidding place.

Now in the heat of battle it loomed through the cannon smoke with the repulsive face of evil.

This was the Devil's Den.

On the rise overlooking this entangled labyrinth was placed the Fourth New York Battery of six guns supported by a brigade holding the southern flank of Birney's division which in itself was guarding the southwest face of Sickles' salient

It was a dangerous place and the danger was not long in coming. Although Hood had complained about the plan of battle, his men hit the Federal line with sledge hammer force, driving the bluecoated infantry back through the dank, rock-walled passages of the Den where much of the fighting was as close as the end of a rifle barrel. The dead and wounded piled up and the sharpshooters held scarlet revelry in the ghostly killing ground.

But it was too much!

Something had to give, and it was the Union line which was forced back leaving the foul ground of the Devil's Den and its overlooking crest and half of the Federal guns in Confederate hands.

The struggle continued.

Just to the north, Longstreet finally turned loose his other division under General Lafayette McLaws to drive headlong against the western face of Sickles' salient, now absorbing the full fury of the Confederate attack.

Part of his division smashed into the Peach Orchard while the rest of it swept along Birney's tenuous line towards a large wheat field abutting the orchard. It was to prove a deadly place for the men of both sides.

To sustain the III Corps in the face of Longstreet's assaults, Meade had been shuttling in units from Sykes' V Corps which had been moved up from the Baltimore Pike where it had been in reserve, a role now to be filled by Sedgwick's VI Corps which had been on the road both night and day.

It was one of these units that broke under the savage blows of McLaws so the fighting lines swept into the

Wheat Field which changed hands six times in charge and countercharge.

Things were beginning to look grim for Meade's army.

It was now close on to six o'clock. Something had to be done to hold the III Corps line. Sickles himself had lost a leg in the fury of the battle.

To bolster the sagging line, General Hancock dispatched a division from the II Corps which arrived just in time to plunge into the Wheat Field battle.

The blue line was holding, but just barely.

It was then McLaws sent in his left flank brigade under General William Barksdale who had been chaffing under restraint. The fiery general led his Mississippians straight for the western face of the salient and the Peach Orchard and the wavering Federal line.

In minutes the yelling Rebels were into the Peach Orchard and the III Corps line along the salient was broken.

A veteran of the Federal forces opposing the attack, would remember the chaos:

"The hoarse and indistinguishable orders of commanding officers, the screaming and bursting of the shells, canister and shrapnel as they tore through the struggling masses of humanity, the death screams of wounded animals, the groans of their human companions, wounded and dying and trampled under foot by hurrying batteries, riderless horses and the moving lines of battle, all combined in an indescribable roar of discordant elements—in fact a perfect hell on earth, never, perhaps to be equaled, certainly not to be surpassed, nor ever to be forgotten in a man's lifetime. It has never been effaced from my memory, day or night, for fifty years."

An aide to General Gibbon in the II Corps lines atop Cemetery Ridge would summarize his thoughts:

"The III Corps is being overpowered. Here and there its lines begin to break—the men begin to pour back to the rear in confusion—the enemy are upon them and among them. Organization is lost to a great degree. Guns and caissons are abandoned and in the hands of the enemy. The III Corps, after a heroic but unfortunate fight, is being literally swept from the field."

But there was one Federal unit that was not being "swept from the field."

That was Andrew A. Humphreys' division of the III Corps which had been deployed along the length of the Emmitsburg Road.

When Birney's line had folded, Humphreys had tucked in his left flank, pulled back his division toward Cemetery Ridge in good order, and offered battle to the enemy.

A cool professional, after his horse was shot seven times, he borrowed another mount to ride the fighting line.

"Twenty times did I bring my men to halt and face about," he told Hancock when at last he got the three thousand survivors of his five-thousand-man division back onto Cemetery Ridge.

He had been first to feel the wrath of A. P. Hill's third corps which now took up Lee's offensive as it developed to the north.

26

Heading for the Gap

THE BATTLE EFFORT OF HILL'S RIGHT HAND DIVISION COM-
manded by Major General Richard H. Anderson
would be more directly at the crest of Cemetery Ridge and
the heart of the Federal main line of defense than the
previous assaults. It would jump off in the dying moments
of the long, bloody day.

And, though the Confederates had no way of knowing
it, that portion of Meade's battle line that had been severely weakened by the detachment of units to stem the
gray tide rolling towards the Round Tops, the Devil's Den,
the Peach Orchard and the Wheat Field would be directly
in its path.

All of the corps, including the VI, still trying to recover
from the effects of its killing forced marches, had contributed to the fight.

But in so doing a gap in the defense line had developed along the crest which would lie squarely in the face of this latest Confederate advance.

First would come the brigades of Wilcox and Lang, hammering at the line Humphreys was trying to hold after the collapse of the salient. But when he had to beat a fighting retreat, the Rebels were on his front and his two flanks, and he had to fall back.

Two more brigades of Anderson's division now joined the attack line, extending even farther to the north. These were the commands of Generals Wright and Posey who, sensing a climactic turn in the fighting, were now coming in for the kill.

"Like the fury of a whirlwind," one II Corps officer saw it. "The whole slope in front is full of them; and in various formations, in line, in column, and in masses which are neither, with yells and thick volleys they are rushing toward our crest."

But Wilcox's men could not be stopped. On they came.

Hancock, commanding that portion of the field for Meade, said:

"In some way five minutes must be gained or we are lost."

He looked about for the means to find only one undersized unit standing on Cemetery Ridge in the face of the oncoming fury.

"What regiment is this?" Hancock called out from his galloping horse.

"The 1st Minnesota," Colonel William Colvill replied.

"Colonel, do you see those colors?" Hancock cried.

"Yes sir," Colvill responded, his eyes on the red battle flag of the Confederacy in the fore of Wilcox' charge.

"Then take them!" Hancock ordered.

And so they did.

Down from the ridge they came into the face of the Rebels.

"Charge bayonets!" Colvill shouted.

The impact of the two lines smashed the force of the charge.

It slowed. It faltered.

Then it stopped.

And slowly, ever so slowly, it began to fall back.

One small regiment in the face of a famous brigade had saved Meade's position. The Minnesotans had answered Hancock's plea.

Wilcox's assault had failed.

But at what cost!

Out of 262 men only 47 would remain fit for combat in the 1st Minnesota.

But Cemetery Ridge would be held for the moment.

Wilcox sent for help.

Would he get it?

He got a curious answer.

The aide had found General Anderson idly chatting with his staff officers on Seminary Ridge.

When his cry for help was heard, the general replied:

"Tell General Wilcox to hold his own, that things will change."

When the disheartened messenger returned to Wilcox he found things would change.

Beset now by Federal troops of the II Corps, both he and Lang to Wilcox's left had but one choice.

The two brigades fell back down the slopes of the ridge.

It was now the turn of Anderson's brigades to the north. They were commanded by Generals Ambrose Wright and Carnot Posey. They advanced promptly.

The assault by Wright's Georgia troops was to be one of the greatest in the entire battle.

Describing it to his wife, he wrote:

"As soon as we emerged from the woods and came into the open fields, the enemy poured a most terrific fire of shells into our ranks. We rushed down the hillside and, reaching the valley, we found it was broken by a series of small ridges and hollows, running parallel with the enemy's line on the mountain, and in the first of these depressions or hollows, our line paused for breath. Then we rushed over the next ridge into the succeeding hollow, and thus we worked our way across that terrible field for more than a mile, under the most furious fire of artillery I had ever seen. When we reached the base of the range upon which the enemy was posted, they opened upon us with their infantry, and raked our whole line with grape and canister from more than twenty guns.

"We were now within a few hundred yards of the enemy's guns, and had up to this time suffered but little loss, the small ridges I have spoken of protecting our men from the enemy's fire, except as we would pass on their tops which we always did in a run, thus exposing ourselves very little to the enemy's fire. But we were in a hot place, and looking to my left through the smoke, I perceived that neither Posey nor Mahone had advanced, and that my left was wholly unprotected. I immediately dispatched a courier to General Anderson informing him of the fact, and he answered that both Posey and Mahone had been ordered in and that he would reiterate the order that I must go on. Before my courier returned, Perry's brigade on my right gave way and shamefully ran to the rear.

"My brigade had now climbed up the side of the mountain nearly to the enemy's guns and, being left without support either on the right or left, enabled the enemy to concentrate a heavy fire upon my small command, but my brave men passed rapidly and steadily on until we approached within fifty or sixty yards of the enemy's batteries, where we encountered a heavy body of infantry posted behind a stone wall. The side of the mountain was so precipitous here that my men could with difficulty climb it, but we strove on, and reaching the stone fence, drove the Yankee infantry from behind it, and then taking cover from the fence we soon shot all the gunners of the enemy's artillery, and rushing over the fence seized their guns. We had now accomplished our task. We had stormed the enemy's strong position, had driven off his infantry, had captured all his guns in our front, except a few which he succeeded in carrying off, and had up to this minute suffered but comparatively little loss.

"Just after taking the enemy's batteries we perceived a heavy column of Yankee infantry on our right flank. They had taken advantage of the gap left in our line by the falling back of Perry's Brigade, and had filed around a piece of timber on our right, and had gotten into the gap left by Perry's brigade and were rapidly getting into our rear. Posey had not advanced on our left, and a strong body of the enemy was advancing down the sides of the mountain to gain our left flank and rear. Thus we were perfectly isolated from any portion of our army a mile in its advance. And although we had gained the enemy's works and captured his guns, we were about to be sacrificed to the bad management and cowardly conduct of others. For a moment I thought all was lost, and that my gallant little band would all be inevitably killed or captured. Colonel Hall of the 22nd had been killed, Colonel Gibson of the 48th seriously wounded, and while at the enemy's guns with his hands on the horses, Major Ross of the 2nd Georgia Battalion had just been shot down. Nearly all my company officers had been killed or wounded. Everything looked gloomy in the extreme, but the men remained firm and cool to the last. The enemy had now gotten completely in our rear, and were advancing upon us over the very ground we had passed in attacking them. A large force concentrated in our front and artillery was brought into position and opened upon us. Then was a prayer said.

"We must face about and cut our way out of the network of bristling bayonets which stretched around us on every side. With cheers and good order we turned our faces to the enemy in our rear, and abandoning our captured guns we rushed upon the flanking column of the enemy and literally cut our way out, and fell back about one-half the distance we had gone over, and then reformed our line. But alas, very few of the brave spirits who so recently had passed over the line buoyant in spirit and confident of success, now answered to the order that calmly sang out upon the air, 'Fall in, Wright's Brigade and here we'll stand again!'"

Here again General Anderson had done nothing to reinforce his spearhead brigade which up until now had scored the greatest success of the day.

At this critical juncture of the battle, Major General Dorsey Pender, commander of A. P. Hill's front line division to the north of Anderson, riding over to see why Mahone of Anderson's division was not supporting Wright, preliminary to ordering his own troops to the attack, was badly wounded by a shell fragment and had to be helped from the field. His next in command failed to move the troops, and no attack was made.

So Wright's penetration of the Cemetery Ridge battle line was hurled back by units of the II and I Corps, hastily flung into the breach to save the Federal line.

With night coming on fast, the action now shifted to the north where Ewell's Second Corps held Lee's battle line running through Gettysburg to the east, facing the bluecoats on Cemetery and Culp's Hills, and around the Federal's right flank and rear, the head and barb of the fishhook.

Old Bald Head had done little to improve the position of his troops during the long morning and afternoon, other than to rearrange some of the batteries of his artillery. But

meanwhile the nervously waiting infantry could see and
hear the bluecoats of Meade's XI and XII Corps strengthening their field fortifications along the crest lines of the two
formidable hills they were waiting to attack.

Finally when the roar of artillery to the south signaled
the opening of Longstreet's long awaited attack, Ewell
ordered his own guns into action. This was the demonstration that Lee had ordered.

He then ordered Early and Johnson forward on the
center and the left of his line, with Rodes on the far right
to exploit any openings uncovered by the two divisions to
the east.

But nothing much happened at first, at least nothing to
prevent Meade from shuffling his troops along Cemetery
Ridge to meet each of the Rebel assaults as they developed.

27

Disappointment in the Twilight

FIRST TO OPEN THE ATTACK AGAINST THE NORTHERN HILLS, was the division of Major General Edward "Allegheny" Johnson on the extreme left of the Confederate battle line.

It was now dusk.

First Lieutenant Randolph McKim of General Steuart's Maryland Brigade remembered:

"It was past six P.M. before our brigade was ordered forward—nearly twenty-four hours after we had gotten into position. We were to storm the eastern face of Culp's Hill, a rough and rugged eminence on the southeast of·the town, which formed the key to the enemy's right center. Passing first through a small skirt of woods, we advanced

143

rapidly in line of battle across a corn field which lay between us and the base of the hill, the enemy opening upon
us briskly as soon as we were unmasked. Rock Creek,
waist-deep in some places, was waded, and now the
whole line, except the 1st North Carolina, held in reserve
on our left flank, pressed up the steep acclivity through
the darkness, and was soon hotly engaged with the enemy.

"After the conflict had been going on for some time, I
ventured to urge the brigadier general commanding to
send forward the 1st North Carolina to reinforce their
struggling comrades. Receiving orders to that effect I led
the regiment up the hill, guided only by the flashes of the
muskets, until I reached a position abreast of our line of
fire on the right. In front, a hundred yards or so, I saw
another line of fire, but owing to the thick foliage could not
determine whether the musket flashes were up or down
the hill. Finding that bullets were whistling over our
heads, I concluded the force in our front must be the
enemy, and seeing, as I thought, an admirable chance of
turning their flank, I urged Colonel Brown to move rapidly
forward and fire. When we reached what I supposed the
proper position, I shouted, 'Fire on them, boys; fire on
them!'

"At that moment Major Parsley, the gallant officer in
command of the 3rd North Carolina, rushed up and
shouted, 'They are our own men.'

"Owing to the din of battle the command to fire had not
been heard except by those nearest to me, and I believe no
injury resulted from my mistake. . . .

"The position thus so hardly won and at so dear a cost
was one of great importance. It was within a few hundred
yards of the Baltimore turnpike, which I think it commanded. Its capture was a breach in the enemy's lines
through which troops might have been poured and the

strong positions of Cemetery Hill rendered untenable. . . .

"It is only in keeping with the haphazard character of the whole battle that the capture of a point of such strategic importance should not have been taken advantage of by the Confederates. It remains, however, no less a proud memory for the officers and men of the 3rd Brigade that their prowess gained for the Confederate general a position where 'Meade's entire line might have been taken in reverse.'

"But if the Confederates did not realize what they had gained, the Federals were fully aware of what they had lost. Accordingly, they spent the night massing troops and artillery for an effort to regain their works. . . . Through the long hours of the night we heard the rumbling of their guns, and thought they were evacuating the hill. The first streak of daylight revealed our mistake. It was scarcely dawn when their artillery opened upon us, at a range of about 500 yards, a terrific and galling fire, to which we had no means of replying, as our guns could not be dragged up that steep and rugged ascent. Then, a little after sunrise, their infantry moved forward in heavy force to attack us. . . .

"They drove in our skirmishers, but could not dislodge us from the works we had captured, although these were commanded in part by the works on the crest of the hill to our right, whence a galling fire was poured into our ranks. Next a strong effort was made to take us in flank, and I well remember that at one time our line resembled three sides of a pentagon, the left side being composed of some other brigade, center and right composed of our own brigade, which thus occupied the most advanced position toward the crest of the hill. About this time, I think, word came to General Steuart that the men's ammunition was almost exhausted. One of his staff immediately took three men and went on foot to the wagons, distant about a mile and a quarter, and brought up two boxes of cartridges 'We emptied each box into a blanket and swung the blanket on a rail, and so carried it to the front.' It was now, I think, about half-past nine, and ever since four o'clock the fire of the enemy had been almost continuous, at times tremendous. . . .

"But all the efforts of the enemy failed to dislodge us. Unassisted, the 3rd Brigade held the position they had won the night before. . . "

Johnson's other two brigades to the right of Steuart's Marylanders didn't do as well as in the darkness. Although attacking savagely, they were too late, for the Federal line, reinforced by troops from the I and XI Corps threw them back three times.

It was now Early's turn to send Hay's Louisiana and Avery's North Carolina Brigades against Cemetery Hill.

When the two brigades left the shelter of some high ground to their immediate front, they drew a crashing fire from the massed Union artillery on Cemetery and Culp's Hills. But they pressed on to begin climbing the slope of the key Cemetery Hill.

Major James Beall of the 21st North Carolina tells the fury of the charge:

"Like an unbroken wave our maddened column rushed on. Four of five color bearers went down. The hour was one of horror."

Then as the advance continued, the men in gray found the Federal guns could not be depressed enough to get at them.

So all of a sudden they were over the crest of Cemetery Hill and into the midst of the Federal artillerymen who fought back with everything they had to hand including rammers and handspikes. Now new blue units were rushed to the breakthrough and the North Carolinians were repulsed.

But in so doing they had left an opening for Hays Louisiana Tigers who captured and silenced the Federal batteries.

For a moment it seemed the Rebels would wrest control of Cemetery Hill out of Federal hands.

Yet again there was not enough weight in the Confederate attack. Without support, Hays had to pull his Tigers back down the hill.

Farther to the right, Ewell's other division under Rodes had with difficulty deployed itself away from the clutter of Gettysburg town. Here again it was too late, for a reconnaissance by brigade commanders showed that the Federals held the western face of the hill in great force. There would be no attack that night on Ewell's far right.

So ended the Second Day at Gettysburg.

Part VI

You can ask me for anything you like, except time.

—Napoleon

28

Midnight War Council

AFULL MOON ROSE OVER THE ENTANGLED BATTLEFIELD where the two armies lay locked in their embrace of death, the silent dead strewn over the fields and slopes where the charges and countercharges had stained the hours with blood.

Wounded men suffered intensely in the July heat, crying for aid or water which would not come. The night brought little surcease from the broiling temperatures of the day.

The southern lines now more closely compressed the Federal position, at this hour confined to Cemetery Ridge and the northern hills.

Over all hung an air of tense expectancy.

Men could not keep doing what they had done on the first two days of the great battle much longer.

There was not much doubt on either side of the lines.

The Third Day would finish it.

Riding back to his headquarters, Lee had no question in his mind as to what the Army of Northern Virginia must do.

It must attack.

Withdrawal after what had happened would be most perilous, if not impossible.

To wait for Meade to attack the army would be equally dangerous in view of its exposed position with all of the problems of supply and communications this far north into Pennsylvania.

The South held good ground for artillery at the Peach Orchard and there were troops to power the assault.

As Lee pondered the three attacks of the day which had almost succeeded—the Round Tops, the penetration of the Cemetery Ridge line, and the assaults on the left at Cemetery and Culp's Hills—he felt certain his men would carry the day.

Back at his headquarters, the orders went out.

The artillery would open as early as possible.

Ewell would send his divisions forward at dawn.

Longstreet would attack the center reinforced with two divisions from Hill's Third Corps.

All the generals concerned knew what they were expected to do.

Would they do it?

Across the dark valley between Seminary Ridge and the Federal position on Cemetery Ridge, the artillery was now silent. So was the infantry but for intermittent flare-ups of outpost firing.

Above all, the moon sailed on through the July night.

With more than twenty thousand of his own men dead,

wounded or missing, Meade felt the terrible weight pressing in upon him.

He was tired. Dead tired.

But Bcb Lee would be tired too.

His killed, wounded and missing would be in the thousands, perhaps even more than Meade's.

Still Meade needed support.

The couriers went out ordering the corps commanders and other generals to a midnight council of war.

For his headquarters, Meade had taken over a tiny farmhouse on the reverse slope just behind the crest of Cemetery Ridge.

There seated at a plain pine-board table sat Meade's chief of staff General Daniel Butterfield, greeting each of the generals as they entered the small, hot room.

Beside him stood the bespectacled George Gordon Meade, commanding general of the Army of the Potomac, looking more like a tired schoolmaster than the chief of the largest army ever mustered on the North American continent.

The candle would gutter as the door opened and closed to admit some of the most famous names on the roster of the United States Army.

There was Winfield Scott Hancock commanding the II Corps, John Newton commanding the dead Reynolds' I Corps, and Henry Slocum of the XII Corps. George Sykes, V Corps; Oliver Otis Howard, XI Corps; John Sedgwick VI Corps; G. K. Warren and John Gibbon. They were all there with others.

The room was heavy with cigar smoke and talk of the day's battles from one end of the line to the other.

Finally Butterfield put an end to the small talk by posing three major questions to the assembled generals.

Should the army retreat or stand where it now was?

If it stayed, should it attack or defend?

If it continued to defend, how long should it wait for Lee's attack?

There was only one answer to the first question. Slocum voiced it: "Stay and fight it out!"

All were agreed the army should continue to defend rather than attack.

To the third question the answers varied—from hours to as long as a day.

Meade summed it up: "The Army would stand and fight."

He added that as Lee had tried both flanks, the third assault would be against the center of the Union line.

After some conversation, the meeting adjourned and the generals returned to their various commands.

They rode back through the sultry silent night, an ironic contrast to the immense sound and violence which had marked the passage of the previous hours.

Meade and Butterfield with the artilleryman Hunt returned to their never ending search for ways to strengthen their lines against the storm which they knew would break on the morrow.

29

An Anxious Dawn

T HE THIRD OF JULY 1863 PROMISED TO BE ANOTHER SWEL-
tering day even before the sun rose over the embattled
lines on Cemetery Ridge.

In the predawn darkness Colonel E. P. Alexander, artillery expert in Longstreet's First Corps,and his staff, had
been engaged in the task of placing the guns to support
the major assault on the Federal lines.

"Before daylight on the morning of the 3rd," he recalled,
"I received orders to post the artillery for an assault upon
the enemy's position, and later I learned that it was to be
led by Pickett's division and directed on Cemetery Hill.
Some of the batteries had gone back for ammunition and
forage, but they were all brought up immediately, and by
daylight all then on the field were posted. Dearing's bat-

155

talion (with Pickett's division) reported sometime during the morning. The enemy fired on our movements and positions occasionally, doing no great damage, and we scarcely returned a shot. The morning was consumed in waiting for Pickett's division, and possibly other movements of infantry. . . ."

While Alexander was moving up his guns, Lee was riding far off to his right to the First Corps headquarters of Longstreet. In the ever growing light he looked in vain for some sign of Pickett's division but could see none.

Dismounting at the corps headquarters, he got the answer fast. It came out of the mouth of Longstreet himself:

"General," he greeted Lee, "I have had my scouts out all night, and I find that you still have an excellent opportunity to move around to the right of Meade's army and maneuver him into attacking us."

His staff even then was drafting orders for his units to move to the south of the Round Tops and take them from that flank.

But although he again listened to Longstreet's arguments, Lee would not change his plans.

He shook his head.

He would attack Meade's center with the First Corps divisions of Hood, McLaws and Pickett, reinforced with other troops.

What Longstreet did not know was that in the darkness his scouts had failed to find two brigades of Sedgwick's VI Corps, sent by Meade to protect his south flank.

But Longstreet had other objections to Lee's plan.

He said later that he replied to Lee:

"General, I have been a soldier all my life. I have been with soldiers engaged in fights by couples, by squads, companies, regiments, and armies, and should know, as well as anyone, what soldiers can do. It is my opinion that no 15,000 men ever arrayed for battle can take that position."

Still finding his commander adamant, he turned to his staff to have them begin preparing the orders.

In a short while, he returned to Lee with more arguments.

Hood's and McLaw's divisions had been badly cut up in yesterday's battle. If they were withdrawn for the attack, Lee's right flank might be in danger.

Lee could accept this.

In place of McLaw's division he would substitute Heth's division of A. P. Hill's Third Corps, now under the command of Johnston Pettigrew, and Hood's division would be replaced by two brigades of Pender's division from the same corps, to be commanded by the fiery Isaac Trimble who had exhibited such displeasure with Ewell's indecision on the first day of the battle.

As this new battle plan would require the movement of two of Hill's divisions, the attack would be delayed until 10 A.M.

A courier was sent galloping off to inform Ewell.

But the change would make no difference to Old Bald Head's troops.

They had been under wicked artillery fire since dawn, the sound of the Federal guns leading Lee's headquarters to believe the roar was that of Ewells' artillery opening on Cemetery and Culp's Hills.

So the battle of Johnson's division on Lee's far left would expend the force he had hoped to use against Meade's right.

Meanwhile Pickett's division had marched southward from the Cashtown Road to an assembly area on the western slopes of Seminary Ridge out of view of the Federal observation posts which had spent the anxious morning examining the Southern lines.

The hours had given time for Sedgwick's weary marchers of the large VI Corps to file into position on the south end of the Cemetery Ridge line behind Sykes' V

Corps where it would constitute Meade's largest reserve force.

So the Federal line ran from the far right: Slocum, Howard, Newton, Hancock, Sedgwick and Sykes.

The weary Meade was as ready for the assault as he ever would be.

30

A Silent Noon

WITH THE SULTRY MORNING GROWING EVER HOTTER, ALexander busied himself with his guns while the thermometer hit 90 degrees. He sent forward 75 of the 83 cannon of the First corps to excellent positions on the Emmitsburg Road reaching north from the Peach Orchard for about 1,300 yards. To the left and rear of this line were posted 60 guns of the Third Corps, with another 24 of Ewell's guns, beyond them.

The Confederates could count about 170 guns, each with from 130 to 150 rounds, to support Pickett's assault.

On the opposite ridge Henry Hunt, Meade's chief of artillery, had placed 77 guns along Cemetery Ridge, with another 50 on Cemetery Hill and Little Round Top, sighted to bring down fire on the approaches to the center of the Federal line.

When the ball opened, there would be plenty of music.

Lee accompanied by the sullen Longstreet twice rode the gray line of infantry brigades with their 47 regiments to ensure that all was in readiness for the attack and that all commanders understood just what they had to do.

Lee's plan for a penetration of Meade's long, battered battle line, was starkly simple.

The battle would open with an artillery preparation delivered by the Confederate guns.

When the Federal batteries had been silenced or their fire appreciably reduced, the infantry lines would cross over the crest of Seminary Hill to begin the great assault designed to break the Army of the Potomac.

The target for the attack would be "a little clump of trees" in the center of Meade's position.

It was now about eleven o'clock with the pitiless sun searing the backs of blue and gray alike.

Skirmishers now decided to provide entertainment for the watching thousands as they quarreled over a house and barn between the grimly waiting armies, setting the buildings afire.

Hill's artillery took the Confederate side for a while but it was a waste of ammunition.

Then all was silent.

It was high noon of a dreadful day to come and men who were there would remember the silence for all their years. That is, if they survived what was to come.

Aside from allowing time for last minute preparations for the ordeal, the silence granted moments of reflection to each man and officer in that vast cathedral of war to ponder on the forces of fate that had brought each of them there.

First, of course, was the matter of life or death.

But in all truth, this chance was not that difficult to contemplate.

For by far most of the men assembled on both sides at Gettysburg were young men.

And for most young men, death is not a threat.

It is a challenge.

And as a challenge it offers a gage to be hurled into the face of the eternal enemy.

Then there was the matter of states' rights. Of regional sovereignty. Of the right to be left alone.

This was a more powerful consideration for the Southerners who truly felt the Union was a union of states which had joined that union by free choice and by the exercise of that free choice were equally free to leave that union when they so desired.

Conversely those from the North felt just as deeply that there was only one Union and that the compact to join that Union was irrevocable.

Finally there was the matter of slavery.

On this issue there was a great deal of ambivalence on both sides.

There it was.

It was wrong.

But what was to be done about it?

Now all of these matters had come to the mark.

These were things that had to be settled one way or the other.

And they were going to be settled.

And what happened here at this little town of Gettysburg would go a long way in effecting this settlement.

Across the valley on Cemetery Ridge the bluecoats dozed in the heat. Soldiers remarked at the strange silence. From time to time the drone of honeybees could be heard.

Meade, who had been working ceaselessly to

strengthen the lines and ensure adequate supplies of ammunition for all units, received a welcome invitation shortly after noon to join General John Gibbon, commander of the 2nd Division of Hancock's II Corps, to have lunch.

When he arrived at a pleasant spot in the shade of a tree near his own headquarters, he found Hancock, Newton, now in command of the III Corps, Alfred Pleasanton, his cavalry commander, and some aides sitting in the grass dining on chicken stew.

It would be an enjoyable interlude.

At the same hour Colonel Alexander in the Confederate guns had received his orders for the bombardment:

"About 12 noon," he recalled, "General Longstreet told me that when Pickett was ready, he would himself give the signal for all our guns to open (which was to be two guns from the Washington Artillery near the center of our line), and meanwhile he desired me to select a suitable position for observation, and to take with me one of General Pickett's staff, and exercise my judgment in selecting the moment for Pickett's advance to begin. Complying, I selected the advanced salient angle of the wood in which Pickett's line was now formed, just on the left flank of my line of 75 guns. While occupying this position and in conversation with General A. R. Wright, commanding a Georgia brigade in A. P. Hill's corps, who had come out there for an observation of the position, I received a note from General Longstreet . . . as follows:

> Colonel:
>   If the artillery fire does not have the effect to drive off or greatly demoralize him so as to make our efforts pretty certain, I would prefer that you should not advise General Pickett to make the charge. I shall rely a great deal on your good judgment to

determine the matter, and shall expect you to let
General Pickett know when the moment offers,
Respectfully,
J. Longstreet, Lieut.-General

"This note at once suggested that there was some alternative to the attack, and placed on me the responsibility of
deciding the question. I endeavored to avoid it by giving
my views in a note, of which I kept no copy, but of which I
have always retained a vivid recollection, having discussed
its points with General A. R. Wright as I wrote it. It was
expressed very nearly as follows:

General:
I will only be able to judge of the effect of our fire
on the enemy by his return fire, for his infantry is
but little exposed to view and the smoke will obscure
the whole field. If, as I infer from your note, there is
any alternative to this attack, it should be carefully
considered before opening our fire, for it will take all
the artillery ammunition we have left to test this one
thoroughly, and if the result is unfavorable, we will
have none left for another effort. And even if this is
entirely successful it can only be so at a very bloody
cost.
Very respectfully, &c.,
E. P. Alexander, Colonel Artillery.

"To this note I soon received the following reply:

Colonel:
The intention is to advance the infantry if the
artillery has the desired effect of driving the enemy's
off, or having other effect such as to warrant us in
making the attack. When that moment arrives advise

General P., and of course advance such artillery as
you can use in aiding the attack.
   Respectfully,
   J. Longstreet, Lieut.-General, Commanding

"This letter again placed the responsibility upon me,
and I felt it very deeply, for the day was rapidly advancing
(it was about 12 noon or a little later), and whatever was to
be done was to be done soon. Meanwhile I had been
anxiously discussing the attack with General A. R. Wright,
who said that the difficulty was not so much in reaching
Cemetery Hill, or taking it—that his brigade had carried it
the afternoon before—but that the trouble was to hold it,
for the whole Federal army was massed in a sort of horse-
shoe shape and could rapidly reinforce the point to any
extent, while our long, enveloping line could not give
prompt enough support. This somewhat reassured me, as
I had heard it said that morning that General Lee had
ordered 'every brigade in the army to charge Cemetery
Hill,' and it was at least certain that the question of supports had had his careful attention. Before answering,
however, I rode back to converse with General Pickett,
whose line was now formed or forming in the wood, and
without telling him of the question I had to decide, I found
out that he was entirely sanguine of success in the charge,
and was only congratulating himself on the opportunity. I
was convinced that to make any half-way effort would
ensure a failure of the campaign, and that if our artillery
fire was once opened, after all the time consumed in preparation for the attack, the only hope of success was to
follow it up promptly with one supreme effort, concentrating every energy we possessed into it, and my mind was
fully made up that if the artillery opened, Pickett must
charge. After the second note from General Longstreet,
therefore, and the interview with Pickett, I did not feel

justified in making any delay, but to acquaint General Longstreet with my determination. I wrote him a note, which I think I quote verbatim, as follows: 'General: When our artillery fire is doing its best I shall advise General Pickett to advance.' It was my intention, as he had a long distance to transverse, that he should start not later than fifteen minutes after our fire opened. . . ."

After sending off his first note to Alexander, Longstreet did a strange thing amid all the tension of expectancy.

During the interchange of notes with Alexander, Colonel Arthur Lyon Freemantle, British Army observer who spent much of that day with Longstreet, stated:

"The general then dismounted and went to sleep for a short time."

In the oppressive heat which enveloped the vast field, men whiled away the minutes in nervous apprehension.

In the nation's capital in Washington, General Henry Halleck in the War Department advised Lincoln, anxiously waiting word in the White House, of a telegram just received from Meade. Sent at 12:30 P.M. it read:

"At the present moment all is quiet."

The president could do nothing but resume his restless vigil.

In Richmond an equally careworn and apprehensive Jefferson Davis waited for news from the North.

31

The Cannon Open

THE SILENT NOON WAS GIVING OVER TO A LONG, HOT deathwatch.

Meade and his generals were finishing their lunch.

Lee and his staff were awaiting the opening of the action.

Soldiers on both sides of the blood-marked valley were still napping in the heat or sitting up to wonder at the uneasy silence which enwrapped them.

It was near on to one o'clock when Longstreet, after closely examining the sweep of the whole vast field through his glasses, wrote a quick note to Colonel J. B. Walton, chief of his corps artillery, and handed it to a courier. It read:

Colonel: Let the batteries open; order great care

and precision in firing. If the batteries in the peach orchard cannot be used against the point we intend attacking, let them open on the rocky hill.
Most respectfully,
J. Longstreet, Lieut.-General Commanding

Walton sent the command to Miller's Third Company of the Washington Artillery which was waiting for it.

Then Lee heard what he was waiting for.

It was the report of a cannon from the Apple Orchard.

Before its sound died away it was followed by a second from the same position.

These were the signal guns.

The bombardment was about to begin.

First came the roar from the Southern guns as one battery after the other sprang into action, shaking the ground with their fury.

General Gibbon's luncheon for Meade suddenly ended as one orderly was killed by flying shell fragments.

From afar could be heard the roar of Hill's Third corps guns to be followed by the distant sound of Ewell's artillery as it joined in the chorus.

On the instant the Federal guns were responding.

The ground trembled while the torrents of sound rolled and echoed over Cemetery Ridge so men had to shout to each other to be understood.

Clods of earth and shards of stone were hurled over the waiting infantrymen from the short rounds while air bursts rained down shell from above.

Federal shell exploded in the trees under which were gathered the long lines of the gray brigades ready for the assault.

Over all soon swirled a cloud of smoke and dust, thick with the smell of gunpowder.

Looking out into the malignant fire storm, Henry Hunt,

Meade's chief of artillery, pronounced it "indescribably grand."

Meade's own headquarters was punished heavily, one shell knocking out the door, almost hitting the army commander. One burst smashed the roof. General Butterfield was wounded.

Headquarters personnel were shortly moved to safer surroundings to the south and east while the reserve artillery and the ammunition trains had to be pulled farther back to the rear.

Colonel Alexander remembers:

"It was 1 P.M. by my watch when the signal guns were fired, the field at that time being entirely silent, but for light picket firing between the lines, and as suddenly as an organ strikes up in a church, the grand roar followed from all the guns of both armies. The enemy's fire was heavy and severe, and their accounts represent ours as having been equally so, though our rifle guns were comparatively few and had only very defective ammunition. . . .

"I had fully intended giving Pickett the order to advance as soon as I saw that our guns had gotten their ranges, say, in ten or fifteen minutes, but the enemy's fire was so severe that when that time had elapsed I could not make up my mind to order the infantry out into a fire which I did not believe they could face, for so long a charge, in such a hot sun, tired as they already were by the march from Chambersburg. . . ."

Across the inferno on Cemetery Hill, Major General Winfield Scott Hancock, commanding the II Corps, rode down his infantry line on his spirited black horse, so that General Abner Doubleday would remember twenty years later:

"I can almost fancy I can see Hancock again, followed by a single orderly displaying his corps flag, while the missiles from a hundred pieces of artillery tore up the ground around him."

When warned that a corps commander should not risk his life in that fashion, Hancock had replied: "There are times when a corps commander's life does not count."

He was showing every soldier in the II Corps that "his general was behind him in the storm."

The Federal artillery was taking fearsome punishment from the Rebel batteries. Men were killed and wounded, caissons were exploded, limbers destroyed. Yet the blue guns kept up a devastating fire on the Confederate battle line.

It was the greatest artillery bombardment ever staged on the North American continent.

Both sides were suffering.

Alexander, watching for a slackening in the fire, wrote:

> I accordingly waited in hopes that our fire would produce some visible effect, or something turn up to make the situation more hopeful; but fifteen minutes more passed without any change in the situation, the fire on neither side slackening for a moment. Even then I could not bring myself to give a peremptory order to Pickett to advance, but feeling that the critical moment would soon pass, I wrote him a note to this effect: 'If you are coming at all you must come immediately or I cannot give you proper support; but the enemy's fire has not slackened materially, and at least 18 guns are still firing from the cemetery itself.'

"This note I sent off at 1:30 P.M., consulting my watch. I afterwards heard what followed its receipt from members of the staff of both Generals Pickett and Longstreet, as follows: Pickett on receiving it galloped over to General Longstreet, who was not far off, and showed it to General L. The latter read it and made no reply. (General Longstreet, himself, speaking of it afterwards, said that he knew the charge had to be made, but could not bring himself to give the order.) General Pickett then said: 'General, shall I advance?' Longstreet turned around and would not answer. Pickett immediately saluted, and said: 'I am going to lead my division forward, sir,' and galloped off to put it in motion; on which General L. left his staff and rode out alone to my position.

"Meanwhile, five minutes after I sent the note to Pickett, the enemy's fire suddenly slackened materially, and the batteries in the cemetery were limbered up and were withdrawn. As the enemy had such abundance of ammunition and so much better guns than ours that they were not compelled to reserve their artillery for critical moments (as we almost always had to do), I knew that they must have felt the punishment a good deal, and I was a good deal elated by the sight. But to make sure that it was a withdrawal for good, and not a mere change of position or relieving of the batteries by fresh ones, I waited for five minutes more, closely examining the ground with a large glass. At that time I sent my courier to Pickett with a note: 'For God's sake come quick; the 18 guns are gone;' and, going to the nearest guns, I sent a lieutenant and a sergeant, one after the other, with other messages to the same effect.

"A few minutes after this, Pickett still not appearing, General Longstreet rode up alone, having seen Pickett and left his staff. I showed him the situation, and said I only feared I could not give Pickett the help I wanted to, my ammunition being very low, and the seven guns under Richardson having been taken off. General Longstreet spoke up promptly: 'Go and stop Pickett right where he is, and replenish your ammunition.' I answered that the ordnance wagons had been nearly emptied, replacing expenditures of the day before, and that not over 20 rounds to the gun were left—too little to accomplish much—and that while this was being done the enemy would recover from the effect of the fire we were now giving him. His reply was: 'I don't want to make this charge; I don't believe it can succeed. I would stop Pickett now, but that General Lee has ordered it and expects it,' and other remarks, showing that he would have been easily induced, even then, to order Pickett to halt.

"It was just at this moment that Pickett's line appeared sweeping out of the wood, Garnett's brigade passing over us."

The great charge had begun.

32

Manning the Line

WAITING OUT THE CANNONADE UNDER THE PROTECTION of reverse slopes or wooded areas, or whatever cover they could find from the showering shot, the impatient Confederate infantrymen were eager for the show to begin.

The long lines of gray were quiet, breaking their silence only once to voice their objections to the appearance of Lee on Traveller in the shell-swept area between the forward guns and their rearward area amid the trees.

But this ceased when the gray horseman doffed his hat in recognition of their fears, and rode out of danger.

In the waiting ranks were gathered the men of 47 of Lee's finest regiments.

On the right of the assault line would be Pickett's division led by the romantic Major General George Pickett, Longstreet's favorite, with his flowing, perfumed hair, but of unquestioned bravery under fire.

His forward right brigade would be that of James Kemper, and the left, that of Richard Garnett, ill, but going into battle with an old blue overcoat wrapped close around him as he sat his big, black horse.

Behind them would be the Third Brigade of General Lewis Armistead, long time friend of the Federal General Hancock from whom he had taken leave before the war started when they were serving in the Old Army at the Pueblo de Los Angeles in far-off California.

To the rear of Pickett would be the redoubtable Cadmus Wilcox whose division would guard the extreme right flank.

Running north from Pickett's troops would be two divisions of A. P. Hill's Third Corps with Heth's division, now commanded by Johnston Pettigrew who had started the battle when he barged into Gettysburg looking for shoes, on Garnett's immediate left flank.

His four brigades would all advance in a front line commanded by Colonel B. D. Fry, Colonel J. K. Marshall, General "Joe" Davis, and Colonel Robert Mayo. These latter two divisions had been badly mauled in the fighting on the first day of the battle.

In their rear would march the two brigades of Pender's division now commanded by the fiery Trimble. They would be led by Colonel William Lowrance and General James Lane. These two brigades had been roughly handled in the first day of fighting.

And they were not only weakened, they were misplaced in the line of battle.

Where Lee had directed they be echeloned out to the

left to provide more weight to the north flank, they instead were placed behind the right and center of Pettigrew's line leaving his left all alone on that flank.

Although Hill had wanted to use his third division, Anderson's, in the assault, Lee had refused, holding it out as his "only reserve."

Fry's would be the center brigade marching straight for the Little Grove of Trees, with all other brigades to the right and left, to dress on Fry once they had emerged into the open ground.

In the battle lines of the attacking regiments numbering some 15,000 men were troops from Virginia, North Carolina, Alabama, Mississippi and Tennessee. If the 47 attacking regiments needed further support, there were troops at hand from South Carolina, Georgia and Florida.

So soldiers from all of the Southern states east of the Mississippi would or could be represented in the assault.

Their wait during the bombardment had been a nervous one, Federal artillery "overs" spraying shell into the trees sheltering the troops, with some bursting over or into the lines themselves.

Across the valley the bluecoated infrantrymen lay waiting, waiting for the grand assault that all knew was coming.

It was now on the way.

Part VII

All hell broke loose.
                                    —John Milton

33

Into the Guns

ALMOST AS IF IN DISDAIN FOR THE NOISE OF THE ARTILLERY
shell shrieking over their heads, the gray lines mustered to their battle posts in silence, all firing or the sounding of the Rebel yell having been forbidden by their commanders.

With their scarlet battleflags fluttering above them, the massed ranks advanced out of the cover of the woods into the swirling smoke and cloud of the hellpit before them.

At the jump-off, Pickett had charged them: "Up, men, and to your posts! Don't forget today that you are from Old Virginia."

For Hill's troops, Pettigrew had shouted to one of his Carolina officers: "Now, Colonel, for the honor of the good Old North State, forward!"

The Confederate batteries fell silent as the troops passed through the guns, the Federal artillery, as if in salute, did likewise.

For moments silence blanketed the great battlefield as it had done at high noon before all the guns had opened.

Longstreet took pride in his troops.

Proudly sitting his horse, he watched them go by:

"Encouraging messages were sent for the columns to hurry on—and they were then on elastic springing step. The officers saluted as they passed, their stern smiles expressing confidence. General Picket, a graceful horseman, sat lightly in the saddle, his brown locks flowing quite over his shoulders. Pettigrew's division spread their steps and quickly rectified the alignment, and the grand march moved bravely on. As soon as the leading columns opened the way, the supports sprang to their alignments. General Trimble mounted, adjusting his seat and reins with an air and grace as if setting out on a pleasant afternoon ride. When aligned to their places, solid march was made down the slope and past our batteries of position.

"Confederate batteries put their fire over the heads of the men as they moved down the slope, and continued to draw the fire of the enemy until the smoke lifted and drifted to the rear, when every gun was turned upon the infantry columns. The batteries that had been drawn off were replaced by others that were fresh. Soldiers and officers began to fall, some to rise no more, others to find their way to the hospital tents. Single files were cut here and there; then the gaps increased, and an occasional shot tore wider openings, but, closing the gaps as quickly as made, the march moved on. . . ."

Clearing the woods, the battle line paused to redress the ranks, then moved on again in parade ground formation.

The Federal guns broke their moment of silence to resume fire with deadly effect on the Confederate advance

stretching for almost a mile in front of the blue can-
noneers.

They made it hell for the gray infantry, but still they
came on.

They were nearing the Emmitsburg Road.

Longstreet, who had dismounted to seat himself on a
rail fence, watched with approving eyes: "The advance was
made in very handsome style," he reported. "All the
troops keeping their lines accurately, and taking fire of the
batteries with great coolness and deliberation."

While he watched, a courier from Pickett came running
up to advise that the enemy's lines would be taken but
reinforcements would be needed.

Immediately orders went out to Wilcox to advance his
brigade forward at once.

The Confederate line had crossed the Emmitsburg Road
and again was pausing to redress the battle line in preparation for the final assault.

Pettigrew's division was now linking up with Pickett's,
although to the far left flank, Mayo's brigade along with
that of Davis was finding it difficult to keep pace with the
others.

Alexander, back at the Confederate artillery positions,
recalled:

"I then galloped along my line of guns, ordering those
that had over twenty rounds left to limber up and follow
Pickett, and those that had less to maintain their fire from
where they were. I had advanced several batteries or parts
of batteries in this way, when Pickett's division appeared
on the slope of Cemetery Hill, and a considerable force of
the enemy were thrown out, attacking his unprotected
right flank. Meanwhile, too, several batteries which had
been withdrawn were run out again and were firing on
him very heavily. We opened on these troops and batteries
with the best we had in the shop, and appeared to do them

considerable damage, but meanwhile Pickett's division just seemed to melt away in the blue musketry smoke which now covered the hill. Nothing but stragglers came back. As soon as it was clear that Pickett was "gone up," I ceased firing, saving what little ammunition was left for fear of an advance by the enemy. About this time General Lee came up to our guns alone and remained there a half hour or more, speaking to Pickett's men as they came straggling back and encouraging them to form again in the first cover they could find."

The final attack was on.

34

AT the Crest

THE GREAT BATTLE HAD NOW REACHED THE CRITICAL point as the massed might of the Confederacy hurled itself at the thin blue line of Hancock's II Corps holding the center of the Cemetery Ridge line in front of that Little Clump of Trees.

The center of Hancock's line was held by his Second Division under the command of a tough fighting man, General John Gibbon.

The general's chief aide was Colonel Frank Haskell, who had done his earlier fighting with the famed Wisconsin Iron Brigade. A Dartmouth man who lived through Gettysburg only to die at the battle at Cold Harbor, he saw it all and was part of it all:

"Half-past two o'clock, an hour and a half since the

commencement, and still the cannonade did not in the least abate; but soon thereafter some signs of weariness and a little slacking of fire began to be apparent upon both sides. . . . All things must end, and the great cannonade was no exception to the general law of earth. In the number of guns active at one time, and in the duration and rapidity of their fire, this artillery engagement, up to this time, must stand alone and pre-eminent in this war. It has not been often, or many times surpassed in the battles of the world. Two hundred and fifty guns, at least, rapidly fired for two mortal hours. . . .

"At three o'clock almost precisely, the last shot hummed, and bounded and fell, and the cannonade was over. The purpose of General Lee in all this fire of his guns—we know it now, we did not at the time so well—was to disable our artillery and break up our infantry upon the position of the II Corps, so as to render them less an impediment to the sweep of his own brigades and divisions over our crest and through our lines. . . . There was a pause between acts, with the curtain down, soon to rise upon the great final act, and catastrophe of Gettysburg. We have passed by the left of the Second Division, coming from the First; when we crossed the crest the enemy was not in sight, and all was still—we walked slowly along in the rear of the troops, by the ridge cut off now from a view of the enemy on his position, and were returning to the spot where we had left our horses. . . . In a moment afterwards we met Captain Wessels and the orderlies who had our horses; they were on foot leading the horses. Captain Wessels was pale, and he said, excited: 'General, they say the enemy's infantry is advancing.' We sprang into our saddles, a score of bounds brought us upon the all-seeing crest.

"To say that men grew pale and held their breath at what we and they there saw would not be true. Might not six thousand men be brave and without shade of fear, and yet, before a hostile eighteen thousand, armed, and not five minutes' march away, turn ashy white? None on that crest now need be told that the enemy is advancing. Every eye could see his legions, an overwhelming resistless tide of an ocean of armed men sweeping upon us! Regiment after regiment and brigade after brigade moved from the woods and rapidly take their places in the lines forming the assault. Pickett's proud division, with some additional troops, hold their right; Pettigrew's (Worth's) their left. The first line at short interval is followed by a second, and that a third succeeds; and columns between support the lines. More than half a mile their front extends; more than a thousand yards the full gray masses deploy, man touching man, rank pressing rank, and line supporting line. The red flags wave, their horsemen gallop up and down; the arms of eighteen thousand men, barrel and bayonet, gleam in the sun, a sloping forest of flashing steel. Right on they move, as with one soul, in perfect order, without impediment of ditch, or wall or stream, over ridge and slope, through orchard and meadow, and cornfield, magnificent, grim, irresistable.

"All was orderly and still upon our crest; no noise and no confusion. The men had little need of commands, for the survivors of a dozen battles knew well enough what this array in front portended, and, already in their places, they would be prepared to act when the right time should come. The click of the locks as each man raised the hammer to feel with his fingers that the cap was on the nipple; the sharp jar as a musket touched a stone upon the wall when thrust in aiming over it, and the clicking of the iron axles as the guns were rolled up by hand a little further to the front, were quite all the sounds that could be heard. Cap-boxes were slid around to the front of the body; cartridge boxes opened, officers opened their pistol-holsters. Such preparations, little more was needed. The

trefoil flags, colors of the brigades and divisions moved to
their places in rear; but along the lines in front the grand
old ensign that first waved in battle at Saratoga in 1777, and
which these people coming would rob of half its stars,
stood up, and the west wind kissed it as the sergeants
sloped its lance towards the enemy. I believe that not one
above whom it then waved but blessed his God that he was
loyal to it, and whose heart did not swell with pride
towards it, as the emblem of the Republic before that
treason's flaunting rag in front.

"General Gibbon rode down the lines, cool and calm,
and in an unimpassioned voice he said to the men, 'Do not
hurry, men, and fire too fast, let them come up close
before you fire, and then aim low and steadily.' The
coolness of their general was reflected in the faces of his
men. Five minutes has elapsed since first the enemy have
emerged from the woods–no great space of time surely, if
measured by the usual standard by which men estimate
duration—but it was long enough for us to note and weigh
some of the elements of mighty moment that surrounded
us; the disparity of numbers between the assailants and
the assailed; that few as were our numbers we could not be
supported or reinforced until support would not be
needed or would be too late; that upon the ability of the
two trefoil divisions to hold the crest and repel the assault
depended not only their own safety or destruction, but
also the honor of the Army of the Potomac and defeat or
victory at Gettysburg. Should these advancing men pierce
our line and become the entering wedge, driven home,
that would sever our army assunder, what hope would
there be afterwards, and where the blood-earned fruits of
yesterday? It was long enough for the Rebel storm to drift
across more than half the space that had at first separated it
from us. None, or all, of these considerations either depressed or elevated us. They might have done the former,

had we been timid; the latter, had we been confident and vain. But, we were there waiting, and ready to do our duty—that done, results could not dishonor us.

"Our skirmishers open a spattering fire along the front and fighting retire upon the main line—the first drops, the heralds of the storm, sounding on our windows. Then the thunders of our guns, first Arnold's then Cushing's and Woodruff's and the rest, shake and reverberate again through the air, and their sounding shells smite the enemy. . . . All our available guns are now active, and from the fire of shells, as the range grows shorter and shorter, they change to shrapnel, and from shrapnel to canister; but in spite of shells, and shrapnel and canister, without wavering or halt, the hardy lines of the enemy continue to move on. The Rebel guns make no reply to ours, and no charging shout rings out today, as is the Rebel wont; but the courage of these silent men amid our shots seems not to need the stimulus of other noise.

"The enemy's right flank sweeps near Stannard's bushy crest, and his concealed Vermonters rake it with a well-delivered fire of musketry. The gray lines do not halt or reply, but withdrawing a little from that extreme, they still move on. And so across all that broad open ground they have come, nearer and nearer, nearly half the way, with our guns bellowing in their faces, until now a hundred yards, no more, divide our ready left from their advancing right. The eager men there are impatient to begin. Let them. First, Harrow's breastworks flame; then Hall's; then Webb's. As if our bullets were the fire coals that touched off their muskets, the enemy in front halts, and his countless level barrels blaze back upon us. The Second Division is struggling in battle. The rattling storm soon spreads to the right, and the blue trefoils are vying with the white. All along each hostile front, a thousand yards, with narrowest space between, the volleys blaze and roll; as thick the sound as when a summer hail storm pelts the city roofs; as thick the fire as when the incessant lightning fringes a summer cloud.

"When the Rebel infantry had opened fire our batteries soon became silent, and this without their fault, for they were foul by long previous use. They were the targets of the concentrated Rebel bullets, and some of them had expended all their canister. But they were not silent before Rhorty was killed, Woodruff had fallen mortally wounded, and Cushing, firing almost his last canister, had dropped dead among his guns, shot through the head by a bullet. The conflict is left to the infantry alone. . . .

"The conflict was tremendous, but I had seen no wavering in all our line. Wondering how long the Rebel ranks, deep though they were, could stand our sheltered volleys, I had come near my destination, when—great heaven! Were my senses mad? The larger portion of Webb's brigade—my God, it was true—there by the group of trees and the angles of the wall was breaking from the cover of their works, and, without orders or reason, with no hand lifted to check them, was falling back, a fear-stricken flock of confusion! The fate of Gettysburg hung upon a spider's single thread!

"A great magnificent passion came on me at the instant, not one that overpowers and confounds, but one that blanches the face and sublimes every sense and faculty. My sword that had always hung idle by my side, the sign of rank only in every battle, I drew, bright and gleaming, the symbol of command. Was not that a fit occasion, and these fugitives the men on whom to try the temper of the Solingen steel? All rules and proprieties were forgotten; all considerations of person, and danger and safety despised; for, as I met the tide of these rabbits, the damned red flags of the rebellion began to thicken and flaunt along the wall they had just deserted, and one was already waving over one of the guns of the dead Cushing. I ordered these men to 'halt,' and 'face about' and 'fire,' and they heard my voice and gathered my meaning, and obeyed my commands. On some unpatriotic backs of those not quick of comprehension, the flat of my sabre fell not lightly, and at its touch their love of country returned, and, with a look at me as if I were the destroying angel, as I might have become theirs, they again faced the enemy.

"General Webb soon came to my assistance. He was on foot, but he was active, and did all that one could do to repair the breach, or to avert its calamity. The men that had fallen back, facing the enemy, soon regained confidence in themselves, and became steady. This portion of the wall was lost to us, and the enemy had gained the cover of the reverse side, where he now stormed with fire. But Webb's men, with their bodies in part protected by the abruptness of the crest, now sent back in the enemies' faces as fierce a storm. Some scores of venturesome Rebels, that in their first push at the wall had dared to cross at the further angle, and those that had desecrated Cushing's guns, were promptly shot down, and speedy death met him who should raise his body to cross it again.

"At this point little could be seen of the enemy, by reason of his cover and the smoke, except the flash of his muskets and his waving flags. These red flags were accumulating at the wall every moment, and they maddened us as the same color does the bull. Webb's men are falling fast, and he is among them to direct and encourage; but, however well they may now do, with that walled enemy in front, with more than a dozen flags to Webb's three, it soon becomes apparent that in not many minutes they will be overpowered, or that there will be none alive for the enemy to overpower. Webb has but three regiments, all small, the 69th, 71st and 72nd Pennsylvania—the 106th Pennsylvania, except two companies, is not here today—

and he must have speedy assistance, or this crest will be lost.

"Oh, where is Gibbon? Where is Hancock?—some general—anybody with the power and the will to support that wasting, melting line? No general came, and no succor! . . . As a last resort I resolved to see if Hall and Harrow could not send some of their commands to reinforce Webb. I galloped to the left in the execution of my purpose, and as I attained the rear of Hall's line, from the nature of the ground and the position of the enemy it was easy to discover the reason and the manner of this gathering of Rebel flags in front of Webb.

"The enemy, emboldened by his success in gaining our line by the group of trees and the angle of the wall, was concentrating all his right against and was further pressing that point. There was the stress of his assault; there would he drive his fiery wedge to split our line. In front of Harrow's and Halls's Brigades he had been able to advance no nearer than when he first halted to deliver fire, and these commands had not yielded an inch. To effect the concentration before Webb, the enemy would march the regiment on his extreme right of each of his lines by the left flank to the rear of the troops, still halted and facing to the front, and so continuing to draw in his right, when they were all massed in the position desired, he would again face them to the front, and advance to the storming. This was the way he made the wall before Webb's line blaze red with his battle flags, and such was the purpose there of his thick-crowding battalions.

"Not a moment must be lost. Colonel Hall I found just in rear of his line, sword in hand, cool, vigilant, noting all that passed and directing the battle of his brigade. The fire was constantly diminishing now in his front, in the manner and by the movement of the enemy that I have mentioned, drifting to the right.

"How is it going?" Colonel Hall asked me, as I rode up. "Well, but Webb is hotly pressed and must have support, or he will be overpowered. Can you assist him?"

"Yes."

"You cannot be too quick."

"I will move my brigade at once."

"Good."

"He gave the order, and in the briefest time I saw five friendly colors hurrying to the aid of the imperiled three; and each color represented true, battle-tried men, that had not turned back from Rebel fire that day nor yesterday, though their ranks were sadly thinned; to Webb's brigade, pressed back as it had been from the wall, the distance was not great from Hall's right. The regiments marched by the right flank . . . The movement, as it did, attracting the enemy's fire, and executed in haste, as it must be, was difficult; but in reasonable time, and in order that is serviceable, if not regular, Hall's men are fighting gallantly side by side with Webb's before the all important point

"I did not stop to see all this movmement of Hall's, but from him I went at once further to the left, to the 1st brigade. General Harrow I did not see, but his fighting men would answer my purpose as well. The 19th Maine, the 15th Massachusetts, the 32nd New York and the shattered old thunderbolt, the 1st Minnesota—poor Farrell was dying then upon the ground where he had fallen—all men that I could find I took over to the right at the double quick.

"As we were moving to, and near the other brigade of the division, from my position on horseback, I could see that the enemy's right, under Hall's fire, was beginning to stagger and to break. 'See,' I said to the men, 'See the chivalry? See the graybacks run!' The men saw, and as they swept to their places by the side of Hall and opened fire, they roared, and this in a manner that said more plainly than words—for the deaf could have seen it in their faces, and the blind would have heard it in their voices— the crest is safe!

"The whole division concentrated, and changes of position, and new phases, as well on our part as on that of the enemy, having as indicated occurred, for the purpose of showing the exact present posture of affairs, some further description is necessary. Before the 2nd Division the enemy is massed, the main bulk of his force covered by the ground that slopes to his rear, with his front at the stone wall. Between his front and us extends the very apex of the crest. All there are left of the White Trefoil Division— yesterday morning there were three thousand eight hundred, this morning there were less than three thousand— at this moment there are somewhat over two thousand;— twelve regiments in three brigades are below or behind the crest, in such a position that by the exposure of the head and upper part of the body above the crest they can deliver their fire in the enemy's faces along the top of the wall.

"By reason of the disorganization incidental in Webb's brigade to his men's having broken and fallen back, as mentioned, in the two other brigades to their rapid and difficult change of position under fire, and in all the divisions in part to severe and continuous battle, formation of companies and regiments in regular ranks is lost; but commands, companies, regiments and brigades are blended and intermixed—an irregular extended mass— men enough, if in order, to form a line of four or five ranks along the whole front of the division. The twelve flags of the regiments wave defiantly at intervals along the front; at the stone wall, at unequal distances from ours of forty, fifty or sixty yards, stream nearly double this number of the battle flags of the enemy.

"These changes accomplished on either side, and the concentration complete, although no cessation or abate-

ment in the general din of conflict since the commencement had at any time been appreciable, now it was as if a
new battle, deadlier, stormier than before, had sprung
from the body of the old—a young Phoenix of combat,
whose eyes stream lightning, shaking his arrowy wings
over the yet glowing ashes of his progenitor. The jostling,
swaying lines on either side boil and rear, and dash their
flamy spray, two hostile billows of a fiery ocean. Thick
flashes stream from the wall, thick volleys answer from the
crest. No threats or expostulation now, only example and
encouragement. All depths of passion are stirred, and all
combatives fire, down to their deep foundations. Individu-
ality is drowned in a sea of clamor, and timid men,
breathing the breath of the multitude, are brave. The fre-
quent dead and wounded lie where they stagger and fall—
there is no humanity for them now, and none can be
spared to care for them. The men do not cheer or shout;
they growl, and over that uneasy sea, heard with the roar
of musketry, sweeps the muttered thunder of a storm of
growls. Webb, Hall, Devereux, Mallon, Abbott among the
men where all are heroes, are doing deeds of note.

"Now the loyal wave rolls up as if it would overleap its
barrier, the crest. Pistols flash with the muskets. My 'Forward to the wall' is answered by the Rebel counter command, 'Steady, men!' and the wave swings back. Again it
surges, and again it sinks. These men of Pennsylvania, on
the soil of their own homesteads, the first and only to flee
the wall, must be the first to storm it. . . . 'Sergeant, forward with your color. Let the Rebels see it close to their
eyes once before they die.' The color sergeant of the 72nd
Pennsylvania, grasping the stump of the severed lance in
both his hands, waved the flag above his head and rushed
towards the wall. 'Will you see your color storm the wall
alone?' One man only starts to follow. Almost half way to
the wall, down go color bearer and color to the ground—

the gallant sergeant is dead. The line springs—the crest of
the solid ground with a great roar heaves forward its
maddened load, men, arms, smoke, fire, a fighting mass.
It rolls to the wall—flash meets flash, the wall is crossed—
a moment ensues of thrusts, yells, blows, shots, and un-
distinguishable conflict, followed by a shout universal that
makes the welkin ring again, and the last and bloodiest
fight of the great battle of Gettysburg is ended and won."

35

Down the Slope

JAMES LONGSTREET WITH HIS PROFESSIONAL SOLDIER'S EYE, saw at once how the tide of battle was moving:
"Colonel Latrobe was sent to General Trimble to have his men fill the line of the broken brigades, and bravely they repaired the damage. The enemy moved out against the supporting brigade in Pickett's rear. Colonel Sorrel was sent to have that move guarded, and Pickett was drawn back to that contention. McLaws was ordered to press his left forward, but the direct line of infantry and cross fire of artillery was telling fearfully on the front. Colonel Fremantle (British army observer) ran up to offer congratulations on the apparent success, but the big gaps in the ranks grew until the lines were reduced to half their length. I called his attention to the broken, struggling ranks. Trim-

ble mended the battle of the left in handsome style, but on the right the massing of the enemy grew stronger and stronger. Brigadier Garnett was killed; Kemper and Trimble were desperately wounded; Generals Hancock and Gibbon were wounded. General Lane succeeded Trimble and with Pettigrew held the battle of the left in steady ranks.

"Pickett's lines being nearer, the impact was heaviest upon them. Most of the field officers were killed or wounded. Colonel Whittle, of Armistead's brigade, who had been shot through the right leg at Williamsburg and lost his left arm at Malvern Hill, was shot through the right arm, then brought down by a shot through his left leg.

"General Armistead, of the second line, spread his steps to supply the places of fallen comrades. His colors cut down, with a volley against the bristling line of bayonets, he put his cap on his sword to guide the storm. The enemy's massing, enveloping numbers held the struggle until the noble Armistead fell beside the wheels of the enemy's battery. Pettigrew was wounded but held his command.

"General Pickett, finding the battle broken while the enemy was still reinforcing, called the troops off. There was no indication of panic. The broken files marched back in steady step. The effort was nobly made and failed from blows that could not be fended."

Colonel Fremantle recalled the action:

"The distance between the Confederate guns and the Yankee position—between the woods crowning the opposite ridges—was at least a mile, quite open, gently undulating, and exposed to artillery the whole distance. This was the ground which had to be crossed in today's attack. Pickett's division, which had just come up, was to bear the brunt in Longstreet's attack, together with Heth and Pettigrew in Hill's corps. Pickett's division was a weak one (under five thousand), owing to the absence of two brigades.

"At noon all Longstreet's dispositions were made; his troops for attack were deployed into line and lying down in the woods; his batteries were ready to open. The general then dismounted and went to sleep for a short time. . . .

"Finding that to see the actual fighting it was absolutely necessary to go into the thick of the thing, I determined to make my way to General Longstreet. It was then about two-thirty. After passing General Lee and his staff, I rode on through the woods in the direction in which I had left Longstreet. I soon began to meet many wounded men returning from the front; many of them asked in piteous tones the way to a doctor or an ambulance. The farther I got, the greater became the number of the wounded. At last I came to a perfect stream of them flocking through the woods in numbers as great as the crowd in Oxford Street in the middle of the day. Some were walking alone on crutches composed of two rifles, others supported by men less badly wounded than themselves, and others were carried on stretchers by the ambulance corps; but in no case did I see a sound man helping the wounded to the rear unless he carried the red badge of the ambulance corps. They were still under a heavy fire; the shells were continually bringing down great limbs of trees, and carrying further destruction amongst this melancholy procession. I saw all this in much less time than it takes to write it, and although astonished to meet such vast numbers of wounded, I had not seen enough to give me any idea of the real extent of the mischief.

"When I got close up to General Longstreet, I saw one of his regiments advancing through the woods in good

order; so, thinking I was just in time to see the attack, I
remarked to the General that 'I wouldn't have missed this
for anything.'

"Longstreet was seated at the top of a snake fence at the
edge of the wood and looking perfectly calm and unper-
turbed. He replied, laughing: 'The devil you wouldn't! I
would like to have missed it very much; we've attacked
and been repulsed; look there!'

"For the first time I then had a view of the open space
between the two positions and saw it covered with Confederates, slowly and sulkily returning toward us in small
broken parties, under a heavy fire of artillery. But the fire
where we were was not so bad as farther to the rear, for
although the air seemed alive with shell, yet the greater
number burst behind us. The General told me that Pickett's division had succeeded in carrying the enemy's position and capturing his guns, but after remaining there
twenty minutes, it had been forced to retire, on the retreat
of Heth and Pettigrew on its left. . . ."

What had happened both on the north and south flanks
of the attack had proven critical to the success of Pickett's
charge.

To the north, the left flank of the Confederate assault ran
into early trouble when Mayo's brigade of Pettigrew's division, delayed at the start of the advance and trying to catch
up, was taken under fire by the Federal artillery of the XI
Corps on Cemetery Hill. With uncertainty in the ranks
while still attempting to regain their place in the line of
battle, Mayo's men were then surprised by an attack on
their left and rear by the 8th Ohio which had been on
skirmish line duty.

The results spelled disaster to the Confederate left flank.
When Mayo's brigade broke under the assault, the Federal
momentum carried the regiment into Davis' brigade, next

in line to the right, furthering rolling up the Rebel left flank.

Likewise to the south, the 13th and 14th Vermont which had taken a position well out to the front of the Cemetery Ridge main line were enabled, along with the 16th Vermont withdrawing from the skirmish line, to unleash a heavy and unexpected blow to Kemper's right and rear, already under fire from the Blue artillery posted on Little Round Top.

Kemper's men, so suddenly beset, crowded north into the brigades of Garnett and Armistead, confusing Pickett's advance into the entangled mass of men which broke the Federal line at The Angle and the Little Grove of Trees.

Even so it was a very near thing for Meade's men.

While the main drama was being played out before Cemetery Ridge, Jeb Stuart and his troopers were taking one last shot at the Army of the Potomac.

Circling to the east around the rear of Ewell's corps, Stuart planned to lead his four brigades of more than six thousand men, first south across the Hanover Road, then west to sever Meade's communications along the Baltimore Pike and the Taney Town Road, get into the rear areas of Meade's army and kill, burn and destroy.

It was a good plan but for one thing.

Two brigades of David Gregg's cavalry division, numbering 45 hundred troopers, were waiting to meet the graycoats at the Hanover Road.

And meet them they did in a savage three-hour battle in which the Federals threw back Stuart's advance to preserve the integrity of Meade's rear areas and communication lines.

The famed cavalryman had drawn another blank.

36

Too bad! Too bad! Oh, too bad!

G EORGE GORDON MEADE RODE UP TO THE CREST TO LOOK
out upon the stricken field strewn with the bodies of
the dead and wounded.

Far down the slope and across the valley to the woodland on Seminary Ridge, he could see the backs of the
retreating enemy.

The Army of the Potomac had won a great victory!

It deserved a loud Hurrah!

Meade, who had doffed his hat, was about to shout it
when he had second thoughts.

Instead he brought his hat down and simply said:
"Thank God!"

Sitting there surveying the field, he was approached by his cavalry chief, General Alfred Pleasonton.

"I will give you half an hour to show yourself a great general," he said bluntly. "Order the army to advance, while I take the cavalry and get in Lee's rear, and we will finish the campaign in a week."

The usually hot tempered Meade replied in a subdued voice.

"How do you know Lee will not attack me again?"

After a pause, he added: "We have done well enough."

In the Southern lines, Colonel Fremantle had left Longstreet:

"Soon afterward I joined General Lee, who had in the meanwhile come to the front on becoming aware of the disaster. If Longstreet's conduct was admirable, that of Lee was perfectly sublime. He was engaged in rallying and in encouraging the broken troops and was riding about a little in front of the wood, quite alone, the whole of his staff being engaged in a similar manner farther to the rear. His face, which is always placid and cheerful, did not show signs of the slightest disappointment, care, or annoyance; and he was addressing to every soldier he met a few words of encouragement, such as: 'All this will come right in the end; we'll talk it over afterwards; but in the meantime, all good men must rally. We want all good and true men just now,' etc. He spoke to all the wounded men that passed him, and the slightly wounded he exhorted to 'bind up their hurts and take up a musket' in this emergency. Very few failed to answer his appeal, and I saw many badly wounded men take off their hats and cheer him.

"He said to me, 'This has been a sad day for us, Colonel—a sad day; but we can't expect always to gain victories.'. . . . I saw General Wilcox come up to him and explain, almost crying, the state of his brigade. General Lee immediately shook hands with him and said cheerfully: 'Never mind, General, all this has been my fault—it is I that have lost this fight, and you must help me out of it in the best way you can.'

"In this way I saw General Lee encourage and reanimate his somewhat dispirited troops and magnanimously take upon his own shoulders the whole weight of the repulse. It was impossible to look at him or to listen to him without feeling the strongest admiration."

Meanwhile, Lee and his generals had to prepare to receive a counterattack from the troops behind those frowning cannon on Cemetery Ridge. Colonel Alexander brought the Confederate artillery from their exposed positions to a new line on Seminary Ridge.

The corps commanders ordered their troops to stronger defensive sites along the crest of the ridge.

But other than an abortive cavalry assault on the far right of Longstreet, the Federals made no move to renew the battle other than to maintain an uncertain artillery fire.

Orders went out to draw the infantry in to shorter lines The enemy did not attempt to interfere.

While the Army of Northern Virginia grimly awaited the attack which did not come, Lee plotted his future course of action. He did not have much choice.

With rations almost gone and the ammunition wagons almost empty, he had but one course open.

Retreat.

Arrangements were put in motion to move out the wounded and the wagon trains.

Hill's Third Corps would lead the combat column, followed by Longstreet's First Corps. Ewell's Second Corps would follow on last.

After conferring with Longstreet, Lee rode on to Hill's headquarters to plan the march.

It was long after midnight when he and Traveller arrived back at his own headquarters.

There he found cavalry general John Imboden awaiting his orders in the moonlight.

The field of Gettysburg was silent.

Wearily he dismounted.

Imboden was sympathetic.

"General, this has been a hard day on you."

"Yes, it has been a sad, sad day for us," Lee replied.

He straightened his tired shoulders.

"I never saw troops behave more magnificently than Pickett's division of Virginians did today in that grand charge upon the enemy," he declared in a spirited voice. "And if they had been supported as there were to have been—but for some reason not yet fully explained to me, were not—we would have held the position and the day would have been ours."

After a moment he went on sadly: "Too bad! Too bad! Oh, too bad!"

37

Exhaustion Takes Command

THE 4TH OF JULY, 1863 SAW THE MORNING LIGHT BREAK over a sad and fearsome field.

Again Gettysburg was ruled by silence.

Not a cannon spoke.

Not even a musket.

But if one listened carefully the low moans of the wounded could be heard from the thousands who lay waiting for help and attention amid the other thousands strewn across the vast battleground, their utter silence testimony to the ferocity of the combat of the afternoon before.

The Southern army was standing to its guns, almost

inviting Meade to send his bluecoats forward into the muzzles of its cannon.

But Meade was too wise—he had had enough.

The butcher's bill had been high.

For the Army of Potomac: A total of 23,049, casualties, 3,155 killed in action, 13,529 wounded, 5,365 missing or captured.

For the Army of Northern Virginia total casualties, 20,451: 2,592 killed, 12,709 wounded and 5,510 missing or captured.

Longstreet spent the early hours watching for signs of a Union attack.

He saw none.

Instead a flag of truce made its way through the bloody field on business concerning the wounded.

When he had finished, the Federal officer announced to the Confederates: "General Longstreet is wounded and a prisoner, but will be taken care of."

Longstreet was amused as he replied that he was neither wounded nor a prisoner.

His laughter echoed over the grim field.

Later in the morning he went to the center of the Confederate lines where the black-mouthed cannon stared across the silent ground. The skies were darkening now, herald of the coming storm.

He asked a young cannoneer, "What o'clock is it?"

The answer came from William Miller Owen of the Washington Artillery. "Eleven fifty-five."

After a short silence, the young artillerist chose to add: "General, this is the 'Glorious Fourth'. We should have a salute from the other side at noon."

They all waited in silence for high noon.

Nothing happened. No guns were fired. No salute.

This was enough for Longstreet.

"Their artillery was too much crippled yesterday to

think of salutes," he said. "Meade is not in good spirits this morning."

About one o'clock rain began to fall from the gathering storm which is said to follow all great battles.

The ambulances and the wagon trains were started for the mountains.

But it was much different in Washington.

For the first three days of the battle the capital had learned little or nothing of what was going on in the hills overlooking the red-bricked town of Gettysburg.

Now after a night filled with rumors that Lee and the Confederates had been badly beaten, the *Washington Star* issued a bulletin at 10 A.M. announcing the great victory.

The town went wild in celebration.

Bands played. Speeches were made. The people cheered.

They cheered again the next day when it was learned that Vicksburg had been surrendered to General Grant on July 4 and the Mississippi, as Lincoln put it, "flowed unvexed to the sea."

But there was no celebrating at Gettysburg.

Napier Bartlett of the Louisiana Washington Artillery remembered the grim morning after the battle, only too well.

"During the whole of this memorable day, and part of the preceding, the men had nothing to eat, and were very often without water. I succeeded at one time in satisfying the pangs of hunger by eating the fruit from a cherry tree, which either hung close to the ground or whose boughs had been struck off by the bullets and shell. The last bread we tasted was obtained by some of us who, to preserve the strength of the men, were detailed by Captain Hero to gather food from the dead Federal infantry, whose haversacks were furnished with three days' ration. It was not the kind of food that fastidious stomachs could endure. But a soldier's first motto is to take care of his material wants, and the men who resolutely satisfied the cravings of nature probably did the best service in marching and fighting, and preserved longest their health.

"The day altogether was productive of different emotions from any ever experienced on any other battle field. The sight of the dying and wounded, who were lying by the thousand between the two lines and compelled amid their sufferings to witness and be exposed to the cannonade of over 200 guns, and later in the day the reckless charges and the subsequent destruction or demoralization of Lee's best corps—the fury, tears or savage irony of the commanders—the patient waiting, which would occasionally break out into sardonic laughter at the ruin of our hopes seen everywhere around us, and finally, the decisive moment, when the enemy seemed to be launching his cavalry to sweep the remaining handful of men from the face of the earth. These were all incidents which settled, and will forever remain in the memory. We all remember Gettysburg, though we do not remember and do not care to remember many other of the remaining incidents of the war. . . .

"But to return to the battle field, from which at a little distance we bivouaced that night. It is true that many of us shed tears at the way in which our dreams of liberty had ended, and then and there gave them a much more careful burial than most of the dead received; yet when we were permitted at length to lie down under the caissons, or in the fence corners, and realized that we had escaped the death that had snatched away so many others, we felt too well satisfied at our good fortune—in spite of the enemy still near us, not to sleep the soundest sleep it is permitted on earth for mortals to enjoy.

"On the following day during a heavy and continuous rain, the army commenced its retreat to the Potomac.

"General Imboden was put in the van in charge of the immense amount of captured plunder, and the many thousand prisoners who had been taken, and our batteries were temporarily assigned to his command. His duty, it need not be said, was a very arduous one, as it exposed us constantly to a sudden swooping down of the cavalry. Once they actually dashed down on us and compelled us to get our pieces unlimbered. Never had the men and horses been so jaded and stove up. One of our men who dropped at the foot of a tree in a sort of hollow went to sleep and continued sleeping until the water rose to his waist. It was only then that he could be awakened with the greatest difficulty. Battery horses would drop down dead. So important was our movement that no halt for bivouac, though we marched scarcely two miles an hour, was made during the route from Gettysburg to Williamsport—a march of over 40 miles. Then men and officers on horseback would go to sleep without knowing it, and at one time there was a halt occasioned by all of the drivers—or at least those whose business was to attend to it, being asleep in their saddles. In fact the whole of the army was dozing while marching and moved as if under enchantment or a spell—they were asleep and at the same time walking.

"Over the rocky turnpike road some of us had to march barefooted, our shoes having been destroyed by the rough macadamized road, or the heavy mud; and those were especially sufferers whose feet, my own among the number, were inconveniently larger than those of the passing Dutchmen whom we would meet on the road.

"Scarcely had we arrived at Williamsport before we were attacked by Kilpatrick with a body of Federal cavalry who had already harassed us at Hagerstown on our retreat, and captured some of our wagons. At Williamsport, the morning after our arrival, there was a sudden dash and hotly contested fight. These assailants were, however, ultimately driven off with the assistance of the wagoners, who now shouldered the muskets they had been hauling and fought like Trojans. In this teamsters' fight, the enemy were driven away without doing any serious damage.

"Lee's army a few days after reached the Potomac without opposition, and although his pontoons were destroyed, and the Potomac unfordable, a bridge was constructed, and the army on the 13th of July passed over very quietly—the bridges having been covered with bushes to prevent the rumbling of the wheels. Ewell's corps by this time had managed to ford the river."

So Lee and his army escaped back to Virginia.

Care for the vast number of wounded in this battle presented major problems for the commanders and the medical services of both sides.

Dr. Jonathan Letterman of the Federal army did his best to meet and solve them.

For Gettysburg he had mustered 3,000 drivers and litter bearers to man his 1,000 ambulances.

Some 650 medical officers were present to care for the troops.

The battle field collection system saw these teams picking up wounded each night within the picket lines and removing them to the field hospitals for care. No distinction in treatment was made between Federals or Confederates.

A total of 14,000 men had been treated by the Union medical services by noon of July 4. The Confederate medical services were rendering the same care on their side of the battle lines.

General Carl Schurz, temporary commander of the Federal XI Corps under Howard, set down his observations of the field hospitals during the battle:

"To look after the wounded of my command, I visited the places where the surgeons were at work. At Bull Run, I had seen only on a very small scale what I was now to behold. At Gettysburg the wounded—many thousands of them—were carried to the farmsteads behind our lines. The houses, the barns, the sheds, and the open barnyards were crowded with the moaning and wailing human beings, and still an unceasing procession of stretchers and ambulances was coming in from all sides to augment the number of the sufferers. A heavy rain set in during the day—the usual rain after a battle—and large numbers had to remain unprotected in the open, there being no room left under roof. I saw long rows of men lying under the eaves of the buildings, the water pouring down upon their bodies in streams. Most of the operating tables were placed in the open where the light was best, some of them partially protected against the rain by tarpaulins or blankets stretched upon poles.

"There stood the surgeons, their sleeves rolled up to the elbows, their bare arms as well as their linen aprons smeared with blood, their knives not seldom held between their teeth, while they were helping a patient on or off the table, or had their hands otherwise occupied; around them pools of blood and amputated arms or legs in heaps, sometimes more than man high. Antiseptic methods were still unknown at that time. As a wounded man was lifted on the table, often shrieking with pain as the attendants handled him, the surgeon quickly examined the wound and resolved upon cutting off the injured limb. Some ether was administered and the body put in position in a moment. The surgeon snatched his knife from between his teeth, where it had been while his hands were busy, wiped it rapidly once or twice across his blood-stained apron, and the cutting began. The operation accomplished, the surgeon would look around with a deep sigh, and then—'Next!'

"And so it went on, hour after hour, while the number of expectant patients seemed hardly to diminish. Now and then one of the wounded men would call attention to the fact that his neighbor lying on the ground had given up the ghost while waiting for his turn, and the dead body was then quietly removed. Or a surgeon, having been long at work, would put down his knife, exclaiming that his hand had grown unsteady, and that this was too much for human endurance—not seldom, hysterical tears streaming down his face. Many of the wounded men suffered with silent fortitude, fierce determination in the knitting of their brows and the steady gaze of their bloodshot eyes. Some would even force themselves to a grim jest about their situation or about the 'skedaddling of the rebels.' But there were, too, heart-rending groans and shrill cries of pain piercing the air, and despairing exclamations, 'Oh, Lord! Oh, Lord!' or 'Let me die!' or softer murmurings in which the words 'mother' or 'father' or 'home' were often heard.

"I saw many of my command among the sufferers, whose faces I well remembered and who greeted me with a look or even a painful smile of recognition, and usually questioning what I thought of their chances of life, or whether I could do anything for them, sometimes, also, whether I thought the enemy were well beaten. I was sadly conscious that many of the words of cheer and encouragement I gave them were mere hollow sound, but they might be at least some solace for the moment."

Women were about the Gettysburg battlefield tending to the wounded shortly after the fighting ended. One of them was 23-year-old Cornelia Hancock of New Jersey, who had answered the call for aid from her brother-in-law Dr. Henry Child of Philadelphia.

She wrote her sister:

Gettysburg—July 8th, 1863

My Dear Sister

We have been two days on the field; go out about
eight and come in about six—go in ambulances or
army buggies. The surgeons of the Second Corps
had one put at our disposal. I feel assured I shall
never feel horrified at anything that may happen to
me hereafter. There is a great want of surgeons here;
there are hundreds of brave fellows, who have not
had their wounds dressed since the battle. Brave is
not the word; more, more Christian fortitude never
was witnessed than they exhibit, always say—"Help
my neighbor first, he is worse." The Second Corps
did the heaviest fighting, and, of course, all who
were badly wounded were in the thickest of the
fight, and, therefore, we deal with the very best class
of the men—that is the bravest. My name is
particularly grateful to them because it is Hancock.
General Hancock is very popular with his men. The
reason why they suffer more in this battle is because
our army is victorious and marching on after Lee,
leaving the wounded for citizens and a very few
surgeons. The citizens are stripped of everything
they have, so you must see the exhausting state of
affairs. The Second Army Corps alone had two
thousand men wounded, this I had from the
Surgeon's headquarters.

I cannot write more. There is no mail that comes
in, we send letters out: I believe the Government has
possession of the road. I hope you will write. It
would be very pleasant to have letters to read in the
evening, for I am so tired I cannot write them. Get
the Penn Relief to send clothing here; there are many
men without anything but a shirt lying in poor
shelter tents, calling on God to take them from this

world of suffering; in fact the air is rent with
petitions to deliver them from their sufferings. . . .

I do not know when I shall go home—it will be
according to how long this hospital stays here and
whether another battle comes soon. I can go right in
an ambulance without being any expense to myself.
The Christian Committee supports us and when they
get tired the Sanitary is on hand. Uncle Sam is very
rich, but very slow, and if it was not for the Sanitary,
much suffering would ensue. We give the men toast
and eggs for breakfast, beef tea at ten o'clock, ham
and bread for dinner, and jelly and bread for supper.
Dried rusk would be nice if they were only here. Old
sheets we would give much for. Bandages are plenty
but sheets very scarce. We have plenty of woolen
blankets now, in fact the hospital is well supplied,
but for about five days after the battle, the men had
no blankets nor scarce any shelter.

It took nearly five days for some three hundred
surgeons to perform the amputations that occurred
here, during which time the rebels lay in a dying
condition without their wounds being dressed or
scarcely any food. If the rebels did not get severely
punished for this battle, then I am no judge. We have
but one rebel in our camp now; he says he never
fired his gun if he could help it, and, therefore, we
treat him first rate. One man died this morning. I
fixed him up as nicely as the place will allow; he will
be buried this afternoon. We are becoming somewhat
civilized here now and the men are well cared for.

On reading the news of the copperhead
performance, in a tent where eight men lay with
nothing but stumps (they call a leg cut off above the
knee a 'stump') they said if they held on a little
longer they would form a stump brigade and go and

fight them. We have some plucky boys in the
hospital, but they suffer awfully. One had his leg cut
off yesterday, and some of the ladies, newcomers,
were up to see him. I told them if they had seen as
many as I had they would not go far to see the sight
again. I could stand by and see a man's head taken
off I believe—you get so used to it here. I should be
perfectly contented if I could receive my letters. I
have the cooking all on my mind pretty much. I have
torn almost all my clothes off of me, and Uncle Sam
has given me a new suit. William says I am very
popular here as I am such a contrast to some of the
office-seeking women who swarm around hospitals.
I am black as an Indian and dirty as a pig and as well
as I ever was in my life—have a nice bunk and tent
about twelve feet square. I have a bed that is made of
four crotch sticks and some sticks laid across and
pine boughs laid on that with blankets on top. It is
equal to any mattress ever made. The tent is open at
night and sometimes I have laid in the damp all
night long, and got up all right in the morning.

The suffering we get used to and the nurses and
doctors, stewards, etc., are very jolly and sometimes
we have a good time. It is very pleasant weather
now. There is all in getting to do what you want to
do and I am doing that. . . .

Pads are terribly needed here. Bandages and lint
are plenty. I would like to see seven barrels of dried
rusk here. I do not know the day of the week or
anything else. Business is slackening a little
though—order is beginning to reign in the hospital
and soon things will be right. One poor fellow is
howling fearfully now while his wounds are being
dressed.

There is no more impropriety in a young person

being here provided they are more sensible than a sexagenarian. Most polite and obliging are all the soldiers to me.

It is a very good place to meet celebrities; they come here from all parts of the United States to see their wounded. Senator Wilson, Mr. Washburn, and one of the Minnesota senators have been here. I get beef tenderloin for dinner.—Ladies who work are favored but the dress-up palaverers are passed by on the other side. I tell you I have lost my memory almost entirely, but it is gradually returning. Dr. Child has done very good service here. All is well with me; we do not know much war news, but I know I am doing all I can, so I do not concern further. Kill the copperheads. Write everything, however trifling, it is all interest here.

From thy affectionate
C. Hancock.

So the two armies began to bind up their wounds as best they could and prepared to fight again.

Part VIII

The semblance of a retreat.
  —*The Richmond Whig,* July 14, 1863

38

Withdrawal and Retreat

IF THE GREAT BATTLE HAD BEEN MARKED BY UNCOORDI-
nated attacks and maneuvers, Lee's withdrawal and
retreat in the face of greatly superior strength was a mas-
terpiece of the military art.

All through the morning and the afternoon the Confederate cannon frowned across from Seminary Ridge re-
minding Meade that where the artillery was there would
be masses of gray infantry to defend the guns.

It was enough.

Not once was an attempt made against the Southern
positions.

When some skirmishers moved forward to the Emmitsburg Road, they were immediately taken under fire from the ridge. They fell back and did not try the same movement again.

This in spite of the fact Colonel Alexander, the artillery expert knew:

"Our ammunition was so low, and our diminished force so widely dispersed along the unwisely extended line, that an advance by a single fresh corps could have cut us in two."

Longstreet's opinion did not agree:

"I had Hood and McLaws, who had not been engaged; I had a heavy force of artillery; I should have liked nothing better than to have been attacked, and have no doubt that I should have given those who tried as bad a reception as Pickett got."

Meade agreed with Longstreet. "I determined not to follow the bad example Lee had set me in ruining himself attacking a strong position."

This statement was made on July 6 when he announced his intention to attack Lee.

But he would only do so, he said, "trusting, should misfortune overtake me, that a sufficient number of my force, in connection with that you (Halleck) have in Washington, could reach that place to render it secure."

So Lee's grim bluff cowed his opponent.

So the two armies faced each other waiting out the noon hour.

At one o'clock the storm broke over the battlefield further hampering arrangements for the trains. But they got underway later in the afternoon. The ambulances and wagons strung out over seventeen miles of highway.

With Imboden and his cavalry guarding the trains, the march of agony proceeded through the storm.

Imboden remembered:

"The rain fell in blinding sheets. Canvas was no protection against its fury, and the wounded men lying upon the naked boards of the wagon-bodies were drenched. Horses and mules were blinded and maddened by the wind and water."

The trains' departure was followed after darkness fell across the field of Gettysburg by the infantry and the artillery units which were to take a shorter route to the Potomac.

After a hellish night and morning, Imboden and his charges dragged their seventeen miles of agony and supplies into Williamsport on the Potomac River late in the afternoon of the next day, July 5. During the retreat the convoy had come under attack by Buford's cavalry division, but it was beaten off handily and the trains came through.

At Williamsport, Imboden learned that Federal cavalry had destroyed the pontoon bridge over which Lee's army was to pass into Virginia. In addition the storm rain had raised the river so the fords were impassable. It was not a pleasant prospect.

Longstreet led the First Corps into Williamsport on the morning of July 6, where Lee greeted his "old war horse" warmly before directing him into the defensive lines his engineers had drawn about the Potomac town.

A. P. Hill's Third Corps followed on in, with Ewell's Second coming last.

The Army of Northern Virginia was together again, prepared to give battle to anyone who would dispute their crossing of the Potomac back onto their home grounds.

It was not until the middle of July 5 that Meade felt able to move.

Timidly he ordered only the VI Corps under Sedgwick to follow on Ewell's heels. But so well did the Confederates do their work that the next morning Sedgwick reported that the pass through the mountains was so well defended that he did not care to "dash my corps against it."

That did it for Meade.

After two days at Gettysburg policing up the battlefield, he moved southward into Maryland to await the arrival of his supply trains.

It was there at his headquarters in the United States Hotel in Frederick that he wrote his wife:

"From the time I took command till today, now over ten days, I have not changed my clothes, have not had a regular night's rest and many nights not a wink of sleep, and for several days did not even wash my face and hands, no regular food, and all the time in a great state of mental anxiety."

In a great state of mental anxiety was Abraham Lincoln, who in this crisis saw an opportunity to destroy Lee's army and perhaps along with Grant's great victory at Vicksburg, bring the Rebellion to an end.

But in spite of all the prodding telegrams from Lincoln and the War Department, Meade would take his time to get ready before he attacked.

In short, staunch fighter that he was, Meade was as intimidated by Lee as all those who had gone before him in command of the Army of the Potomac: McClellan, Pope, Burnside and Hooker.

He would only move when he felt assured of victory.

Lee started moving his wounded over the Potomac but the troops and trains would have to wait behind the field fortifications which extended in a wide semi-circle to protect Williamsport and Falling Waters. There still was no attack by Meade's forces.

The pursuit dragged on into July 13 when Lee was moving Ewell's and Longstreet's corps across the river, only to be beset by another savage rainstorm which made the roads, deep with mud, almost impassable. But the troops got across both by fords and by a make-shift pontoon bridge which had been built by Major J. A. Harmon, Jackson's old quartermaster.

Only Hill's corps, bringing up the rear, got into trouble when the Federal cavalry attacked. But they were beaten off by Heth's division which had started the Battle of Gettysburg in the first place.

Finally the Southern army, but for a few of the rear guard, had passed over the Potomac.

Lee heaved a great sigh of relief.

In the White House at Washington, Robert Lincoln found his father in tears, his head in his arms.

When he asked why, the President replied:

"My boy, when I heard that the bridge at Williamsport had been swept away, I sent for General Haupt and asked him how soon he could replace the same. He replied, 'If I were uninterrupted I could build a bridge with the material there within twenty-four hours, and Mr. President, General lee has engineers as skilful as I am.' Upon hearing this I at once wrote Meade to attack without delay, and if successful to destroy my letter, but in case of failure to preserve it for his vindication. I have just learned that at a council of war of Meade and his generals, it has been determined not to pursue Lee, and now the opportune chance of ending this bitter struggle is lost."

With these words the Gettysburg Campaign and Lee's invasion of the North, came to an end.

39

Letters: Sent and Unsent

WITH HIS ARMY SAFELY BACK IN VIRGINIA AT ORANGE Courthouse, south of the Rapidan River, Lee reviewed the campaign in a lengthy letter to President Davis in Richmond.

Under date of July 13, he wrote in conclusion:

> The army in my opinion achieved under the guidance of the Most High a general success, though it did not win a victory. I thought at the time that the latter was practicable. I still think if all things would have worked together it would have been accomplished. But with the knowledge I then had, and in the circumstances I was then placed, I do not

know what better course I could have pursued. With my present knowledge, and could I have foreseen that the attack on the last day would have failed to drive the enemy from his position, I should certainly have tried some other course. What the ultimate result would have been is not so clear to me.

Three weeks later he again write Davis a more fateful letter:

> Camp Orange, August 8, 1863
> His Excellency Jefferson Davis, President of the Confederate States:
> Mr. President: Your letters of July 28 and August 2 have been received, and I have waited for a leisure hour to reply, but I fear that will never come. I am extremely obliged to you for the attention given to the wants of this army, and the efforts made to supply them. Our absentees are returning, and I hope the earnest and beautiful appeal made to the country in your proclamation may stir up the virtue of the whole people, and that they may see their duty and perform it. Nothing is wanted but that their fortitude should equal their bravery to ensure the success of our cause. We must expect reverses, even defeats. They are sent to teach us wisdom and prudence, to call forth greater energies, and to prevent our falling into greater disasters. Our people have only to be true and united, to bear manfully the misfortunes incident to war, and all will come right in the end.
> I know how prone we are to censure and how ready to blame others for the non-fulfillment of our expectations. This is unbecoming in a generous people, and I grieve to see its expression. The general remedy for the want of success in a military

commander is his removal. This is natural, and, in many instances, proper. For, no matter what may be the ability of the officer, if he loses the confidence of his troops disaster must sooner or later ensue.

I have been prompted by these reflections more than once since my return from Pennsylvania to propose to Your Excellency the propriety of selecting another commander for this army. I have seen and heard of expression of discontent in the public journals at the result of the expedition. I do not know how far this feeling extends in the army. My brother officers have been too kind to report it, and so far the troops have been too generous to exhibit it. It is fair, however, to suppose that it does exist, and success is so necessary to us that nothing should be risked to secure it. I therefore, in all sincerity, request Your Excellency to take measures to supply my place. I do this with the more earnestness because no one is more aware than myself of my inability for the duties of my position. I cannot even accomplish what I myself desire. How can I fulfill the expectations of others? In addition I sensibly feel the growing failure of my bodily strength. I have not yet recovered from the attack I experienced the past spring. I am becoming more and more incapable of exertion, and am thus prevented from making the personal examinations and giving the personal supervision to the operations in the field which I feel to be necessary. I am so dull that in making use of the eyes of others I am frequently misled. Everything, therefore, points to the advantages to be derived from a new commander, and I the more anxiously urge the matter upon Your Excellency from my belief that a younger and abler man than myself can readily be attained. I know that he will have as gallant and brave an army as ever existed to second his effort, and it would be the happiest day of my life to see at its head a worthy leader—one that would accomplish more than I could perform and all that I have wished. I hope Your Excellency will attribute my request to the true reason, the desire to serve my country, and to do all in my power to ensure the success of her righteous cause.

I have no complaints to make of any one but myself. I have received nothing but kindness from those above me, and the most considerate attention from my comrades and companions in arms. To Your Excellency I am specially indebted for uniform kindness and consideration. You have done everything in your power to aid me in the work committed to my charge, without omitting anything to promote the general welfare. I pray that your efforts may at length be crowned with success, and that you may long live to enjoy the thanks of a grateful people.

With sentiments of great esteem, I am, very respectfully and truly, yours,

R. E. Lee,
General

Lee's answer was not long in forthcoming from Davis:

Richmond, Va., August 11, 1863
General R. E. Lee, Commanding Army of Northern Virginia:

Yours of 8th instant has been received. I am glad that you concur so entirely with me as to the want of our country in this trying hour, and am happy to add that after the first depression consequent upon our disaster in the west, indications have appeared that our people will exhibit that fortitude which we agree in believing is alone needful to secure ultimate success.

It well became Sidney Johnston, when overwhelmed by a senseless clamor, to admit the rule that success is the test of merit; and yet there has been nothing which I have found to require a greater effort of patience than to bear the criticisms of the ignorant, who pronounce everything a failure which does not equal their expectations or desires, and can see no good result which is not in the line of their own imaginings. I admit the propriety of your conclusions that an officer who loses the confidence of his troops should have his position changed, whatever may be his ability, but when I read the sentence I was not all prepared for the application you were about to make. Expressions of discontent in the public journals furnish but little evidence of the sentiment of an army. I wish it were otherwise, even though all the abuse of myself should be accepted as the results of honest observation. I say I wish I could feel that the public journals were not generally partisan nor venal.

Were you capable of stooping to it, you could easily surround yourself with those who would fill the press with your laudations, and seek to exalt you for what you had not done, rather than detract from the achievements which will make you and your army the subject of history and object of the world's admiration for generations to come.

I am truly sorry to know that you still feel the effects of the illness you suffered last spring, and can readily understand the embarrassments you experience in using the eyes of others, having been so much accustomed to make your own reconnaissances. Practice will, however, do much to relieve that embarrassment, and the minute knowledge of the country which you have acquired will render you less dependent for topographical information.

But suppose, my dear friend, that I were to admit, with all their implications, the points which you present, where am I to find that new commander who is to possess the greater ability which you believe to be required? I do not doubt the readiness with which you would give way to one who could accomplish all that you have wished, and you will do me the justice to believe that if Providence should kindly offer such a person for our use, I would not hesitate to avail of his services.

My sight is not sufficiently penetrating to discover such hidden merit, if it exists, and I have but used to you the language of sober earnestness when I have impressed upon you the propriety of avoiding all unnecessary exposure to danger, because I felt our country could not bear to lose you. To ask me to substitute you by some one in my judgment more fit to command, or who would possess more of the confidence of the army, or of the reflecting men of the country, is to demand an impossibility.

It only remains for me to hope that you will take all possible care of yourself, that your health and strength may be entirely restored, and that the Lord will preserve you for the important duties devolved upon you in the struggle of our suffering country for the independence which we have engaged in war to maintain.

As ever, very respectfully and truly, yours,

Jefferson Davis

So, Lee had his orders and the war would go on. In Washington a frustrated Abraham Lincoln had writ-

ten a sharply critical letter to Meade on his failure to pin
Lee up against the flooded Potomac and destroy him.

Beset with angry grief, he told his secretary, John Hay:
"We had them within our grasp. We had only to stretch
forth our hands and they were ours. And nothing I could
say or do could make the army move."

But the letter was never sent, Lincoln apparently feeling
that it would do little good.

Meade, hearing of the president's anger, sent in a hot
letter of resignation. But General Halleck held it up,
soothed the ruffled general, and Meade received a promo-
tion to the grade of brigadier general in the Regular Army
as a reward for his services at Gettysburg.

The war would go on.

40

The Benediction

WITH HIS ARMY RECOVERING ITS STRENGTH IN VIRGINIA while Meade watched him with a wary eye from the northward, Lee began planning another campaign to carry the war to the enemy.

But it was slow going and indecisive, like two boxers sparring their way around a ring.

August dragged its way into September with no action other than the friction generated by the picket lines and cavalry patrols where they rubbed up against each other at the far edges of the armies.

Finally Lee felt strong enough to move.

He would maneuver Meade out of his position on the Rapidan and then once he had flushed him into the open, he would attack him. The odds would be with the Federals—they always were.

229

But through his spies he had learned that Meade had been forced to detach XI and XII Corps for duty in the West, just as he had sent Longstreet and his First Corps to duty in Tennessee.

It was early October and the nights were long and chill.

Still the Army of Northern Virginia was full of fight as it marched northward once again.

But Meade would have nothing to do with Lee. His Army of the Potomac pulled back from the Rapidan, recrossed to the north side of the Rappahannock and awaited Lee's further moves.

They were not long in coming, so on October 14 a heavy action was fought by the two armies at a place called Bristoe Station. Once again it was Heth's division of A. P. Hill's Third Corps attacking their old antagonists of Gettysburg, the Union II Corps fighting without their bold commander, the gallant Hancock, now convalescing from the severe wounds he had sustained in the action along Cemetery Ridge.

The Federals got the better of the action, with Hill taking the blame for a mismanaged battle.

Lee's reply was as chilly as the autumn air. He told Hill:

"Well, well, General, bury these poor men and let us say no more about it."

At the same time, his cavalry reported Meade's army was entrenching behind Bull Run, barely twenty miles from Washington.

Deciding he had gone as far as he could go, Lee turned his troops southward to beyond the Rapidan.

Except for one indecisive action, the campaign of 1863 was over.

But there remained one more ritual of war to be performed.

It would be the dedication of a National Cemetery at Gettysburg to be held on November 19.

The site would be near the place where the Confederate infantry had charged into Howard's XI Corps artillery, not far to the north of The Little Clump of Trees on Cemetery Ridge.

The *New York Times* headlined its story:

"THE HEROES OF JULY. A solemn and Imposing Event. . . . Immense Numbers of Visitors. Oration by Hon. Edward Everett—Speeches of President Lincoln, Mr. Seward and Governor Seymour."

It reported on the ceremonies under command of Major General Couch, with the march moving through the streets of Gettysburg, beginning at 10 o'clock, to the speakers' stand on the heights above the town:

"Although a heavy fog clouded the heavens in the morning during the procession, the sun broke out in all its brilliancy during the Rev. Mr. Stockton's prayer and shone upon the magnificent spectacle. The assemblage was of great magnitude, and was gathered within a circle of great extent around the stand, which was located on the highest point of ground on which the battle was fought. A long line of military surrounded the position taken by the immense multitude of people. . . ."

Under a subhead entitled "President Lincoln's Address," the two-column front page story, then printed those words which every American has heard or read:

Fourscore and seven years ago our Fathers brought forth upon this continent a new nation, conceived in liberty and dedicated to the proposition that all men are created equal. (Applause) Now we are engaged in a great civil war, testing whether that nation, or any nation so conceived and so dedicated, can long endure. We are met on a great battle-field of that war We are met to dedicate a portion of it as the final resting place for those who here gave their lives that

that nation might live. It is altogether fitting and
proper that we should do this. But in a larger sense
we cannot dedicate, we cannot consecrate, we cannot
hallow this ground. The brave men, living and dead,
who struggled here have consecrated it far above our
power to add or detract. (Applause) The world will
little note nor long remember what we say here, but
it can never forget what they did here. (Applause) It
is for us, the living, rather to be dedicated here to the
unfinished work that they have thus far so nobly
advanced. (Applause) It is rather for us to be here
dedicated to the great task remaining before us, that
from these honored dead we take increased devotion
to that cause for which they gave the last full
measure of devotion; that we here highly resolve that
these dead shall not have died in vain (Applause)
that this nation under God shall have a new birth of
freedom, and that government of the people, by the
people, and for the people, shall not perish from the
earth. (Long continued applause.)

Three cheers were then given for the President and
the Governors of the States.

41

Controversy and Contention

BUT THE BATTLE ITSELF WOULD NOT DIE.
Of all the many actions fought by American soldiers, in all the many wars engaged in by the nation, no other battle than Gettysburg has given rise to so much controversy and contention.

It started almost as soon as the last shot was fired over that famous battle ground.

It was because of hearing or reading some of this that Lee was prompted to write his letter of resignation to Jefferson Davis.

No Southern general including Lee, himself, escaped the storm of debate generated by the struggle.

Longstreet, Stuart, Ewell and Hill, all had their critics or defenders, while some of the arguments involved brigade and regimental commanders.

On the Northern side, Meade, Sickles, Howard and Doubleday did not escape unscathed.

But as the battle was deemed a Federal victory, they fared much better than their southern counterparts.

In all of this, Lee took no part either during the war or after. He wrote no memoirs or recollections of the struggle. Neither did he criticize nor derogate any of his subordinate officers.

Until he died, he was a warm friend and admirer of Longstreet, who, himself, was one of the chief targets of Southern censure for his actions or lack of action during the battle.

It was in the South, after the surrender at Appomattox, that the criticism boiled around Lee's "Old Warhorse."

The more Gettysburg was seen as the watershed battle after which the Southern fortunes continued to slide towards eventual defeat, the more the controversy swelled

It continued on into the twentieth century, and as a matter of fact, can be said to have never ended, as many of the details of the great battle are still under contention today.

Involved as much as the characters and actions of the major participants is the fascinating interplay of time and events as the battle unfolded to its conclusion. Such great stakes were sometimes dependent on such narrow margins of time, or such minor happenings, that it seems as if fate itself were taking a hand in playing out this most critical of all American armed struggles.

The greatest stake of all, of course, was the future destiny of the United States of America.

Never up until that time had that future been in any doubt.

And never afterwards would that destiny be at hazard

until the seventh of December of 1941, when in the course of a single day the future of the nation would be dependent on the actions of other men over which she had no control.

The peace party in the North, in the wake of a series of Federal defeats, had continued to gather strength, so that the future of Abraham Lincoln and his party in the elections of 1864 was in doubt.

A great Southern victory at Gettysburg would provide a major obstacle to the further conduct of the war by the North.

Likewise, foreign intervention by the European powers, chiefly Britain and France, which had come so close in 1862, would receive new life from a Confederate victory.

Then there was the North itself.

If Lee could break Meade's army in half, there would be little left to stand between him and the capture of Washington or Baltimore, or even the City of Philadelphia.

These were some of the greatest prizes Lee had in mind when he sent his Army of Northern Virginia swinging north into Pennyslvania in June of 1863.

Conversely, the South needed to win to live.

Lee knew better than anyone else that to stand on the defensive and invite the enemy's attack in Virginia was a no-win policy which in the end could only result in the defeat of an enfeebled Confederacy.

The South already was beginning to feel the constrictions of shortages of food and forage, of money and of men. If she could not win a victory of major magnitude, then the ultimate loss of the great Rebellion would be certain.

On a more mundane level, an invasion of the North would lift the great burden of two huge armies off the ravaged fields of Virginia, and transfer it to the fat and rich farmlands of the North.

In addition such a campaign would forestall any invasion of the suffering Southland by the Army of the Potomac.

These were the major forces impelling him to the North.

Could it be done?

He and his Army of Northern Virginia would come close to doing it!

Very close indeed!

Part IX

For of all sad words of tongue or pen, the saddest are these: It might have been!

—Whittier

42

The Critical Points

IN ITS DEVELOPING ACTION, GETTYSBURG PRESENTS FOUR critical points where, if the chain of events had swung the other way, the final decision could have resulted in a Confederate victory or a Union defeat.

First and perhaps the most critical of all developed at the inception of the campaign in Virginia when Lee had finished his preliminary planning and was ready to launch his thunderbolt at Meade's army and the North itself.

This was the still unexplained disappearance of Lee's most trusted intelligence chief, General Jeb Stuart, and his three finest brigades of cavalry from their assembly areas south of the Potomac, not to reappear again until the second day of the great battle of Gettysburg.

In their absence Lee was deprived of the "eyes and ears"

of the army and Stuart himself, perhaps the greatest intelligence officer in the whole war other than Lee himself.

This left Lee to feel his way blindly into Pennsylvania, to stumble into the battle in total ignorance of the positions or strength of the Army of the Potomac coming hard to wreck his formations and his plans.

Second critical point was on the first day of the battle when Ewell, coming in on the left of A. P. Hill, captured the town of Gettysburg and thus was presented with the opportunity to seize Cemetery Hill south of the town, the dominant terrain feature of the entire battlefield.

Third critical point was the failure of the Confederates to seize the Round Tops and the southern flank of the Cemetery Ridge line on the second day of the battle.

Fourth critical point was at the climax of the great battle when Lee launched his most massive blow to break the Federal line. Pickett's charge would be outrageously delayed. It would not be delivered in the formation designed by Lee. It would not be properly supported. And it would fail.

43

Stuart Loses the Army

WHEN THE FLAMBOYANT YET IMMENSELY TALENTED CAV-alryman General Jeb Stuart pondered Lee's specific orders of June 22 and 23 at the beginning of the invasion of the North, he found that he was assigned his major mission in both sets of instructions.

That of June 22 read:

> Do you know where he (Hooker) is and what he is doing? I fear he will steal a march on us, and get across the Potomac before we are aware. If you find that he is moving northward, and that two brigades can guard the Blue Ridge and take care of your rear, you can move with the other three into Maryland, and take position on General Ewell's right, place

yourself in communication with him, guard his
flank, keep him informed on the enemy's
movements, and collect all the supplies you can for
the use of the army.

To make sure that there could be no mistake, Lee wrote
again on June 23:

If General Hooker's army remains inactive, you can
leave two brigades to watch him, and withdraw with
the three others, but should he not appear to be
moving northward, I think you had better withdraw
this side of the mountains tomorrow night, cross at
Shepherdstown next day, and move over to
Frederickstown.
You will, however, be able to judge whether you
can pass around their army without hinderance,
doing them all the damage you can, and cross the
river east of the mountains. In either case, after
crossing the river, you must move on and feel the
right of Ewell's troops, collecting information,
provisions, etc.
. . I think the sooner you cross into Maryland,
after tomorrow, the better.

Lee's orders of June 22 were relayed to Stuart through
Longstreet who added this note:

General Lee has inclosed to me this letter for you,
to be forwarded to you provided you can be spared
from my front, and provided I think that you can
move across the Potomac without disclosing our
plans. He speaks of your leaving, via Hopewell Gap,
and passing by the rear of the enemy. If you can get
through by that route, I think that you will be less

likely to indicate what your plans are than if you
should cross by passing to our rear. I forward the
letter of instructions with these suggestions. . . . P.S.
I think that your passage of the Potomac by our rear
at the present moment will, in a measure, disclose
our plans. You had better not leave us, therefore,
unless you can take the proposed route in rear of the
enemy.

So Stuart had to be careful to guard the secrecy of the
army's movement of the three corps across the Potomac by
allowing no maneuver of the cavalry to unmask Lee's plan
for the invasion of the north.

In any event, if Stuart was to find Hooker was not
"moving northward," Lee had written: "I think you had
better withdraw this side of the mountains tomorrow
night, cross at Shepherdstown next day . . ." in the track
of the main invasion.

Stuart, who had been smarting from criticism in the
South over his indecisive action with the Yankee cavalry at
Brandy Station the day after his theatrical review of his five
brigades of Confederate horse, saw in these orders the
opportunity to score a major blow at the enemy.

He was to express his evaluation of the orders:

"In the exercise of the discretion vested in me by the
commanding general, it was deemed practical to move
entirely in the enemy's rear, intercepting his communications with his base, and, inflicting damage upon his rear,
to rejoin the army in Pennyslvania in time to participate in
its actual conflicts."

So at one o'clock in the morning of June 25, he put his
brigades in motion eastward to pass through Glasscock's
Gap in the Bull Run mountains, then to turn to the north,
inflicting whatever damage he could to the enemy before
rejoining the army on Ewell's flank.

But upon emerging through the gap and leaving the
Bull Run mountains behind, the graycoated troopers
found the long columns of Hancock's II Corps moving
northward on the same roads Stuart had intended to use.

It was the moment of critical decision.

Should the cavalry turn back to the westward to come
trotting up on the rear of Longstreet's First Corps making
for the Potomac crossings, or should it take the more
adventuresome and daring course of continuing around
the rear of Hancock's II Corps and ride northward between
the Army of the Potomac and Washington before joining
Ewell in Pennsylvania?

The thrust of Lee's orders was that his first priority was
to take position on Ewell's right flank if Hooker was crossing the river. But how could one know that the movement
of Hancock's corps indicated a crossing?

Only if he could "pass around their army without hindrance" could he continue on around the Federals and so
on to the north.

It would seem that his encounter with one of the finest
fighting corps in the Union Army would be a hindrance.

But Jeb did not see it that way.

He and his troopers had ridden around the Army of the
Potomac twice before when it was under the command of
McClellan, the first time in June of 1862 during the Penin-
sular Campaign in front of Richmond, and the second
time in October after the battle of Antietam.

A third great raid was too much for the dashing Jeb to
resist.

It would be done.

Besides Lee had given him the discretion and he would
use it.

The great prestige of the graycoated cavalry would be
restored.

In any event he and his troopers would take their

proper station on the right flank of Ewell in plenty of time for any major action in Pennsylvania.

The orders went out.

The gray brigades would continue on eastward seeking for the gap through which they could ride north.

On June 26, while Stuart was still heading for a ford on the Potomac, Early's division of Ewell's corps had captured Gettysburg some 80 miles to the north. Lee himself was with Hill in Chambersburg, 30 miles west of Early.

The commanding general was mildly concerned with the absence of all dispatches from Stuart who was usually so prompt and so timely with his reports.

Still the invasion must proceed as planned.

No news was good news!

On June 27, Ewell was still advancing in two columns. One had captured Carlisle, home of the old U. S. Army cavalry barracks, the other, to the south under Early, was close to York.

But what of Stuart?

He was preparing to cross over the Potomac, his advance proceeding heavily because of tired horses and hungry men.

By the 28th, Lee was growing more and more apprehensive that either some harm had befallen Stuart and his troopers, or that Hooker had turned his army towards the south and Richmond.

His own advance through Pennsylvania was now growing more dependent with each passing hour on accurate information as to the location of the enemy's major units and their movement or lack of movement.

But of this, he knew nothing.

Still Ewell must keep moving forward, his immediate objective the capital of Pennsylvania, Harrisburg, and the bridges across the broad waters of the Susquehanna River.

Longstreet and Hill would follow on the next day.

Anxiety and frustration caused by lack of intelligence of the enemy, and news of the position and movement of Stuart and his brigades, were now beginning to exert their toll on the usual calm behavior of the commanding general. He was tending to show his irritation with small matters that had gone awry, and some observers felt that he looked unwell.

On this day Stuart's men fell upon an eight-mile long Federal wagon train making its way with supplies from Washington to the Army of the Potomac. Capture of 125 wagons loaded with foodstuffs and forage, and the destruction of many more, was easy work for the veteran troopers, but all of this consumed precious hours during which their primary mission to "take position on General Ewell's right . . . guard his flank . . . keep him informed of the enemy's movements," went unfulfilled and forgotten.

It was late on this night that Lee, who had retired in an agony of fear for the safety of Stuart and his command and apprehension over the whereabouts and movement of Hooker's army corps, was awakened to be confronted by the spy Harrison with his unsettling news that the Army of the Potomac with its new commander, General Meade, had crossed the Potomac and was now hot on the heels of the Army of Northern Virginia.

Plans for the invasion of the North began to collapse on the instant.

Danger was in the wind.

Lee, ever the realist, responded immediately.

The army must gather itself.

Shortly, galloping couriers were speeding the orders through the night.

Ewell would be recalled from his advance through Pennsylvania.

Hill and Longstreet would speed their march.

In the absence of Stuart, the two cavalry brigades left behind in Virginia must come north with speed.

The point of concentration would be either of the small towns of Cashtown or Gettysburg.

The gods of war would decide which.

Stuart, all unaware of the crisis which was tightening its grip on the army, continued his plodding march to the north.

Yet he certainly must have been uneasy over the days now running into five, during which he had sent not one bit of intelligence to his commanding general.

Outwardly he showed no sign of concern.

Nor did he seem concerned over the fatigue of his men and their mounts as the plodding ride went on.

To make up time, he had ordered the command to move during the night hours, further compounding the state of inertia which now began to overcome almost everyone but himself.

Slowly the whole nodding column moved into the sixth day of the expedition.

Finally after eight days, Stuart stood before Lee who could barely restrain his anger. It was the second day of the great battle.

Yet what was done was done. The lost days could not be recalled.

In the end, Lee forgave his erring lieutenant.

But the damage, and it was great, had been devastating

The invasion had been destroyed.

The army had stumbled into the Army of the Potomac not knowing where the Federal combat units were, nor in what strength.

Thousands of Confederate dead lay strewn on the slopes of McPherson's and Seminary Ridges as a result of the blundering advance.

What had happened to Stuart, the intelligence officer without peer?

That question has never been answered.

44

Cemetery Hill—First Day

WHEN HARRY HETH'S DIVISION OF A. P. HILL'S THIRD Corps, flung out its skirmishers along the forward slopes of Herr Ridge to deliver its attack on the bluecoated troopers scattered along McPherson's Ridge in the misty dawn of July 1, 1863, nobody really thought there would be any real obstacle to the Confederates' objective to get into Gettysburg to buy some shoes.

That is nobody but the cold-eyed Union cavalry commander John Buford, who had holed up along the woods and ridgeline to discourage any such shopping expedition.

Immediately upon getting his troops into a blocking position, he sent word back to General John Reynolds, commander of Meade's left wing, that Gettysburg was the place for battle, and that he would have to have support if he was to halt the attacks that Heth was throwing at his undermanned line.

Reynolds, never the one to hestitate, started units of the I and XI Corps forward, then rode on to the front to see for himself. Once there he asked Buford if he could hold until the troops came up and Buford assured him he could.

Reynolds was leading these troops to the ridge when he was cut down by a Confederate sharpshooter.

Yet his troops held and were still there blocking Heth's advance when General Lee rode on the field.

Heth, who was under instructions from A. P. Hill, sick in the rear at Cashtown, rode up to report to Lee that a very bloody engagement lasting from morning until afternoon had failed to shake the Federals. While they were talking, Rodes' division of Ewell's Second Corps had swept out of the woods to the north, taken the Federal lines before Gettysburg by surprise and the troops holding up Heth on their flanks.

Lee, who had told Heth not to renew his attack because he was not ready to bring on a general engagement, then unleashed him at the enemy to exploit the unexpected success.

Beset on the front and on the flank, the McPherson Ridge line began to bend and then to break.

Fighting stubbornly, the bluecoats were beaten off McPherson's Ridge to retreat to Seminary Ridge. But they had not been there long when a new thrust delivered by Dorsey Pender's division of Hill's corps broke their line again, and the retreat to the protection of the hills south of Gettysburg began.

North of the town, where Rodes' men had now been joined by Jubal Early's division, also of Ewell's corps, the Southern attack was sweeping all before it.

Gettysburg was lost to the blue infantrymen who were now making their way singly, in groups, and in columns towards Cemetery Hill and Cemetery Ridge, south of the town.

What had been a withdrawal was turning into a rout.

Lee wanted Hill's corps to renew the attack and capture Cemetery Hill, but the corps commander who was pale and sick demurred. Heth's and Pender's men were exhausted. They could not carry the heights.

But someone would have to.

Lee could see that Cemetery Hill dominated the whole hill mass south of the town with the exception of Culp's Hill which rose above it over to the east.

If Hill could not capture this key terrain feature, then it would have to be Ewell's task.

He sent Major Walter Taylor of his staff galloping off to the left to report his findings to the beak-nosed Ewell.

"General Ewell . . . was instructed to carry the hill occupied by the enemy, if he found it practicable, but to avoid a general engagement until the arrival of the other corps of the army which were ordered to hasten forward," Lee said.

With this message, Taylor rode into the middle of a boiling controversy.

General John B. Gordon of Early's division had started it.

Halted while pursuing the Federals in his front, he felt that an immediate attack, before they could gather their forces, would give the Confederates Cemetery Hill and perhaps the battle.

He rode over to Ewell's field headquarters, to urge such action, to find his commander sitting quietly on his mount.

Expecting to receive instant orders to attack, he heard nothing.

Gordon in tense silence waited for Ewell to speak. But not a word was uttered.

While they sat their mounts on that hot afternoon in Gettysburg, an aide arrived to report that Ewell's third division under command of "Allegheny" Johnson was close to Gettysburg and upon arrival would be ready to go into action.

This was too much for the battle-fired Gordon who broke in to state that his men were ready to join Johnson's attack. Cemetery Hill would be in Southern hands before nightfall.

It was close to four o'clock in the afternoon with some four full hours of daylight left in this fateful day.

But Ewell ignored Gordon to tell Johnson's aide that the division should continue to advance until well to the front when it should be halted for further orders.

Listeners were amazed at Ewell's apparent indecision.

This was the soldier who had been one of Stonewall Jackson's chief lieutenants.

Now at this critical moment in the war, he could not make up his mind.

Then with Gordon with him, he decided to ride into the town where they were brought under rifle fire. Several men went down and Ewell was hit.

Gordon cried out in alarm: "Are you hurt, sir?"

Ewell replied calmly that it did no harm to be hit in a wooden leg.

The pair then rode on to the town square where Ewell talked to some of his soldiers.

Still no action.

Because of the firing in the town, the general was urged to a safer place for his headquarters.

It was here that his volunteer aide, General Isaac Trimble, came to advise immediate attack. But he received no affirmative response.

An officer observing Ewell's inaction, recalled:

"It was a moment of most critical importance, more evidently critical to us now, than it would seem to any one then. But even then, some of us who had served on Jackson's staff, sat in a group in our saddles, and one said sadly, 'Jackson is not here.' Our corps commander. . . . was simply waiting for orders when every moment of the time could not be balanced with gold."

But he did have to place Johnson's division when it took its position in the line.

Even in this he wanted the advice of Early, who had been in Gettysburg the week before on their way north.

When Early arrived at the field headquarters, he urged an immediate attack, but seeing Ewell was not disposed to move, he held his tongue.

Now another distraction arose when it was reported a column of Federals was moving in on his left flank. Early discounted these reports as mere rumors.

But Ewell had to see for himself.

So with Early and Rodes, who had reported that he had not pressed his successful attack on Seminary Ridge on to Cemetery Hill because his division had been weakened in its first attack on the Federal lines, and also because he had been advised that Lee did not wish to bring on a general engagement, Ewell rode out to the left where a good view could be had of the York Road.

Yet even then the three generals could not agree.

Rodes saw Federals on both sides of the highway.

Early scoffed at the idea of the enemy on that flank.

Ewell was neutral.

With the sun nearly down, Early went back to his own command in some disgust at the inaction, while Ewell and Rodes returned to the headquarters. There they learned that Johnson's division was coming in to Gettysburg and that the men they had seen on the York Road off to the left flank were Confederate troops after all.

In the gathering dusk, Lee was dismounting after riding over from the center of the long Confederate line.

The council of war that followed was a mournful affair.

Lee immediately saw that Ewell had no intention of attacking Cemetery Hill that night. More troublesome, he sensed that his responsibilities in commanding the Second Corps might be proving to be too much for him.

So Lee opened the agenda for the next day by asking Ewell: "Can't you, with your corps, attack on this flank at daylight tomorrow?"

He never got a chance to reply, for Early, who had ridden in to join the war council, spoke up first.

He was against a frontal assault on Cemetery Hill, saying the approaches were difficult and would make any such advance a most costly one. Instead, he argued, the attack should come from Longstreet's front against the Round Tops whose shapes were rapidly fading into the night.

With Early and Rodes in agreement with their corps chief, Lee then proposed he move the Second Corps around to the right to shorten the lines of the army and put more power into the center.

But here again, strangely, Lee encountered opposition from Early who did not want to give up a foot of ground. His argument was that when the army attacked on its right, the Second Corps then could deliver a flanking attack on the Federal positions and roll up their line.

Again Ewell and Rodes contented themselves with going along with the outspoken Early.

Lee was bewildered, if not shaken. Here were the heirs to Jackson's doctrine of offense, all ready to have his old corps accept a passive role in the battle.

After a while Lee acquiesced.

Longstreet would open the second day of the battle with an assault from the right, with the Second Corps demonstrating against the Federals and ready to exploit all the opportunities that the First Corps attack might unfold.

Wearily, Lee mounted Traveller to return to the headquarters of the Army through the moonlight which eerily illuminated the ghastly field.

Once Lee was back at his headquarters he began to have second thoughts about the plan he had agreed upon with Ewell. Very bluntly, he was afraid the burden of the battle would be placed entirely on the First and Third Corps with the Second Corps sitting passively on the sidelines.

He sat down and sent a message back to Ewell that the ground on the right looked favorable to an attack, and that he should move over to the right during the night so the army could hit with all its force.

But something had happened.

Ewell mounted up and came over to Lee's headquarters.

He reported two of his lieutenants had scouted Culp's Hill and had found no Federal troops.

Ewell said that he felt if he stayed where he was, Johnson's division could capture that dominating height.

After hearing Old Bald Head out, Lee agreed. Culp's Hill with Confederate cannon atop it could make Cemetery Hill and Cemetery Ridge untenable for the Federal army.

It was agreed then that Ewell would seize Culp's Hill as soon as he could do so.

Longstreet was present at all the discussion which ended when Ewell rode away to return to the Second Corps.

With the clock getting on towards midnight, a courier was dispatched after the beleagured general with orders not to attack until he had heard the sound of Longstreet's opening guns.

Before retiring for a few hours sleep or rest, Lee announced to his bone weary staff officers: "Gentlemen, we will attack the enemy as early in the morning as practicable."

But Ewell would have a different problem.

Riding into his headquarters to order Johnson to attack and seize Culp's Hill, he found "Allegheny" had already tried to do so but his troops had been thrown back by Federals on the hill.

In addition, he was shown a captured Federal dispatch which showed that the V and XII Corps of the Army of the Potomac were closing on Gettysburg.

By then it was too late for Jackson's lieutenant to do anything to change the course of fate, for he could see the first signs of the new day.

There had been another council of war that night of July 1.

After Hancock had reported to Meade on the awful events of the first day of battle, at Meade's headquarters in Taneytown about nine o'clock Meade mounted up and rode to the blood-drenched front.

Arriving after midnight on the crest of Cemetery Hill, he called a conference at the house of the gatekeeper of the cemetery which gave its name to the hill. After the meeting got underway, he turned to Howard of the XI Corps, which had taken such a beating during the day.

"Well, Howard," Meade said, "what do you think? Is this the place to fight the battle?"

Howard looked at his commanding general.

"I am confident we can hold this position," he replied.

His other senior officers present agreed.

"I am glad to hear you say so," Meade said. "I have already ordered the other corps to concentrate here—and it is too late to change."

So a few hours of darkness brought an uneasy quiet to the vast battlefield.

But they did not bring peace of mind to Ewell.

He had failed, and he knew he had failed.

The golden opportunity had fled.

The second day of the great battle was about to open.

45

The Round Tops—
Second Day

O N THE CRITICAL MORNING OF JULY 2, 1863, THE SECOND
day of the great battle, Lee, who had had a few hours
rest in a little house north of the Chambersburg Road, was
up and about long before daylight which would not come
to Gettysburg until 4:32 A.M.

About 4 o'clock he sent Captain Samuel Johnston, an
Engineer officer, off to survey the terrain over which the
attack on the Federal left and center was to take place.

Shortly after this he was at his observation post on
Seminary Ridge, examining through his glasses evidence
of the Federal strength revealed by the growing light
spreading across Cemetery Ridge.

But little could he see of troops south of those gathered on Cemetery and Culp's Hills. Apparently Meade was still concentrated in opposition to where he had been so savagely attacked by Hill and Ewell on the northern end of the Gettysburg line.

Yet Lee knew from the captured Federal dispatch that Sykes' V Corps and Slocum's XII Corps were even then forcing their marches to bring their troops into their battle positions on the Cemetery Ridge line.

Of his own troops: Hill and Ewell were already in position where they had left off the fight on the previous day. McLaws' division, which was leading Longstreet's First Corps, had halted at midnight about two miles from Gettysburg. It was under orders to march into its battle positions beginning with the dawn. Hood's division was following in the immediate rear, with the artillery bringing up the march.

So all of his force with the exception of Pickett's division which was still on the road should be closed and ready for deployment by 9 A.M.

Lee, mindful of the great need for speed in delivering the attack before the blue lines were in position to meet him, was most anxious that preparations for the coming battle be pressed.

He was joined at his observation post sometime after five o'clock by Longstreet and A. P. Hill, and shortly after by Hood and other generals.

The march of the divisions, however, was slow and they were probably not in position and not deployed for battle until well after nine o'clock.

On the Federal side, however, faced with the desperate need to fill in their battle lines, the marches were forced so that Hancock's II Corps started to extend and strengthen its assigned positions along the crest of Cemetery Ridge to the south a little after seven o'clock. The II Corps was followed shortly by the arrival of the III Corps on the line, with the V Corps filing in an hour later.

Where Meade had barely 20,000 fit-for-duty men, mostly on Cemetery and Culp's Hills at daybreak, the fast-marching Federals had increased this number to some 58,000 by nine o'clock.

Lee, who so desperately knew the need for speed, was slowly but surely losing the advantages he had scored in his swift concentration followed by the Confederate victory on the first day of battle.

While Lee waited for the First Corps to move into their battle positions, Longstreet continued his argument for a turning movement around the left of the Federal line. Lee listened but he found Old Pete's plans impracticable.

His practiced eye had found two excellent artillery positions, one west of LIttle Round Top and one in a peach orchard along the Emmitsburg Road, from which Southern gunners could assist the infantry assault.

A successful assault by Ewell on Cemetery Hill would further increase the odds of a Southern victory.

In need of solitude, Lee left the congregation of generals and foreign observers to walk alone under some trees.

It was then Longstreet had observed to Hood, "The General is a little nervous this morning; he wishes me to attack; I do not wish to do so without Pickett. I never like to go into battle with one boot off."

Pickett's division, of course, would not arrive on the battlefield until late in the afternoon at the earliest.

Previously Lee had told Hood:

"The enemy is here and if we do not whip him, he will whip us."

When McLaws came up to report his troops ready for movement and after Lee had explained his tactical plan to the general, Longstreet directly contradicted Lee's instructions on the placement of McLaws' division.

A puzzled McLaws then returned to his troops while Lee mounted up to ride over to Ewell's front, leaving Longstreet to simmer out his antagonism, and to finally get his attack underway.

But his ride accomplished little other than to impress on Ewell the need to exploit any advantages he could find once his demonstration had opened upon the sound of Longstreet's guns.

Upon his return, when he found Longstreet had done little to further the assault, he had to directly order him to do so.

By then the sun was high overhead.

But there would be still more delays.

When Captain Johnston, who had been detailed to guide the march, reported that the original route crossed a rise where the troops would be seen from Cemetery Ridge, but that he had found a better way, Longstreet would not hear of it, deciding instead to countermarch by a long and devious way, which would not bring Hood's and McLaws' troops into their attack positions for another hour and a half.

Then Hood's scouts had discovered a way to flank the Round Tops, but again Longstreet would not listen. The attack would go in as Lee had ordered forthwith.

The same answer would be given to McLaws when he discovered the III Federal Corps of Daniel Sickles deployed in the Peach Orchard along the Emmitsburg Road over which he had been ordered to attack. Longstreet differed, saying there was only a single regiment and a battery in that position. When asked by McLaws to come see for himself, Longstreet had roughly refused.

In addition, none of this latest information on the changing enemy positions was passed on to Lee.

The attacks would go in with explosive force but not

nearly with the same effect as if they had been adjusted to the changing conditions.

As it was, Sickles' III Corps would be almost destroyed in its exposed position, far in advance of the main Federal defense line, a mistake which Meade had discovered too late to do anything about.

Little Round Top would be held momentarily by one of Hood's regiments before being driven off.

The Peach Orchard, the Devil's Den and the Wheat Field would all be in Southern hands by nightfall.

Then two brigades of Anderson's division of Hill's Third Corps would charge into the Federal artillery on Cemetery Ridge. But they lacked adequate support and would be driven back. The lack of support would result in charges that the division commander, Anderson, was "indifferent to his duties" in these climactic charges on the second day at Gettysburg.

Then as the battle action moved north along the line, troops from two of Ewell's divisions would, in uncoordinated attacks, capture portions of Cemetery Hill and Culp's Hill before being driven back by counterattacks.

So in spite of Longstreet's delays, Ewell's hesitation, A. P. Hill's inability because of sickness to properly direct his corps in action, and Stuart's unexplained absence, the rank and file of the Army of Northern Virginia had captured vital ground on the battlefield, and inflicted great damage on the Army of the Potomac.

There is little wonder then that Lee felt that he had an excellent chance to rupture the Federal line with an attack of penetration on the following day.

Such an attack, if successful, should result in the rout of Meade's army, and then, who could know? Washington, Baltimore or Philadelphia would be wide open to advancing Southern arms.

Across the valley on Cemetery Ridge, now swathed in the bright light of the July full moon, George Gordon Meade had called his own council of war of his corps commanders, artillery and cavalry commanders, and other generals.

It had been a desperate and fearful day.

The question put to the generals crowding the main room, thick with cigar smoke, of the small farm house, just behind the crest of Cemetery Ridge where it looked across the valley at the enemy host licking its wounds after the bloody day, was a simple one.

What should the Army of the Potomac do?

Attack, defend, or retreat?

Slocum, commander of the XII Corps, answered Meade. "Stay and fight it out!"

As the meeting was breaking up, Meade turned to General Gibbon who had taken over the II Corps command from General Hancock, who would command that portion of the field.

The II Corps was in the middle of the Cemetery Ridge line.

"If Lee attacks tomorrow," he said, "it will be on your front."

Gibbon looked at Meade steadily, as Meade went on:

"He has made attacks on both our flanks and failed, and if he concludes to try it again, it will be on our center."

The stage was set.

46

The Little Clump of Trees—Third Day

THE BLISTERING HOT SUN WHICH SEARED THE DEADLY battlefield on July 3, 1863, would forever be remembered by the many thousands who fought there.

If hell were an oven, Gettysburg would be a fiery furnace at the forge of the gods of war.

After a night of but little, fitful sleep, Lee once again rode in the early dawn over to his right flank where he expected to find Pickett's division and other units of the First and Third Corps preparing for the grand assault which would penetrate and rupture that frowning blue line on the opposite ridge.

Already he could hear the roar of Ewell's guns to the

north, but he could not know that the Second Corps brigades were involved in a bloody, fruitless effort to extend their positions on Culp's Hill from which they would be driven before the morning was out.

So the planned flanking attack by Ewell to assist Longstreet's smash at the Union center would abort into meaningless but brutal fighting which would wear itself out before the main attack would get underway.

At Longstreet's headquarters he quickly learned there would be more delays.

For Old Pete claimed that his scouts had found the Federal left "in the air" and was at the moment drafting plans for a movement to his own right.

Once again Lee had to patiently explain that he would attack Meade in his center, and that Longstreet would deliver that attack.

Then Longstreet had maintained that Hood's and McLaw's divisions which had been mauled on the second day of battle could not attack from their present positions, and could not be withdrawn without imperiling the flank and rear of the First Corps.

So once again Lee had been forced to redraw his battle plans, replacing Longstreet's men with troops from Hill's Third Corps. This entailed further delay so the morning was well advanced when the infantry were finally in position to deliver the great assault.

By this time the fighting around the hills in front of Ewell had died away, and the strange silence of Gettysburg enwrapped the uneasy contestants in unreal quiet.

Three times he rode Traveller along the long lines of waiting infantry and artillerymen, twice with Longstreet and once alone.

At his final conference with Longstreet and Hill, he checked with his commanders if all details of the attack were clearly understood.

They were.

Shortly after one o'clock the signal guns had been fired and the Southern artillery had opened, to be joined almost immediately in throaty challenge by the Federal guns on the long line running from Cemetery Hill, along Cemetery Ridge and ending with those on Little Round Top.

The thunder of the guns shook the Pennsylvania hills while veterans of the battle would remember the shock of the cannonade so long as they should live.

Destruction and killing were immense in numbers of men, horses, guns and ammunition.

It would be the greatest artillery bombardment in the history of the American continents.

Then would come the pause as the grayclad host gathered itself for the charge which, although men could not see it then, would decide for all time the course of this Civil War.

When the Confederate assault wave broke into the blue lines and guns on Cemetery Ridge the issue would be in terrible doubt. But it could not be sustained and would be repelled, leaving the survivors to make their melancholy way back to the shelter of their own lines.

The Little Clump of Trees, target of the attack directed by Lee, would mark the high tide of the Confederacy.

In the end it had failed.

But it was so close.

So very, very close.

Part X

If you have tears, prepare to shed them now.
—Shakespeare

47

The Last Muster

G ETTYSBURG, FOR ALL ITS SMOKE AND FLAME AND
thunder and carnage, was not at the time perceived
as the climactic battle of the war.

Other terrible battles were to follow in the eastern the-
ater of the war: The Wilderness, Spotsylvania, Cold Harbor and Petersburg.

But none of these would grip the emotions of the people, both North and South, as Gettysburg.

After the war had ended and the years rolled on, the
great battle came to be seen as the turning point, the pivot
after which the fortunes of the South commenced their
downturn which would only end in Lee's surrender at
Appomattox.

Bitter acrimony in the South began to gather about the
conduct of the battle and the actions of the various com-

manders on those three fatal days of July 1, July 2, and July 3, 1863.

Lee, who, after the surrender at Appomattox, accepted the presidency of Washington College in Lexington, Virginia, held himself aloof from any controversy about the battle.

But that did not discourage some of the principal actors in the traumatic struggle.

General Jeb Stuart was the first.

On July 10, 1863, he wrote his wife:

"My cavalry has nobly sustained its reputation, and done better and harder fighting than it ever has since the war."

But he was slow to file his official report. When it finally came to Colonel Charles Marshall, Lee's aide de camp and the military secretary who prepared the first draft of official reports of operations, it was long and detailed.

At its conclusion, he listed the reasons which, in his opinion, justified his long and unexplained, at the time, absence from the army which had blindfolded Lee on his crucial advance into the North.

Stuart maintained he had put Washington on the defensive; that he had drawn the Federal cavalry away from the Confederate flanks at Williamsport and Hagerstown; he had harassed Sedgwick's VI Corps, delaying its arrival at Gettyburg; he had slowed Meade's advance; and his actions in the overall had protected Lee's trains better than if he and his men had tried to block the many mountain passes.

He wrote:

"If the peculiar functions of the cavalry with the army were not satisfactorily performed in the absence of my command, it should rather be attributed to the fact that Jenkins' brigade was not as efficient as it ought to have been, and as its numbers (3,800) on leaving Virginia warranted us in expecting."

Marshall told Stuart it would have been better for the command if he "had obeyed orders."

But Lee would not go that far.

In his official report on the battle, he wrote that Stuart's decision to cross the Potomac between the Army of the Potomac and Washington was "in the exercise of the discretion given him."

As to Stuart's failure to execute his main mission, Lee commented:

"He was instructed to lose no time in placing his command on the right of our column as soon as he should perceive the enemy moving northward."

As a result of not so doing, Lee wrote:

"The movements of the army preceding the battle of Gettysburg had been much embarrassed by the absence of the cavalry."

That ended the matter officially, but words could not buy back the precious days wasted on the rambling expedition up through Maryland and Pennsylvania when Lee should have been receiving reports from Stuart on the changing dispositions of the Federal corps as they pursued him on his advance to the north.

Stuart would continue his distinguished career through the bloody months ahead in the shell-torn reaches of the Wilderness and the crimson fields at Spotsylvania.

In these great battles of the 1864 campaign, he would be facing a new antoagonist in Major General Phil Sheridan, commander of the Federal cavalry under the new Union general-in-chief, Ulysses S. Grant, who had left his great victories in the West to come East to finish the war.

General Meade would continue to lead the Army of the Potomac but in the public's mind, because the new general would make his headquarters with that force, it would in fact become "Grant's army."

Hammering through the Wilderness, the bluecoats were advancing on the Spotsylvania Court House when Stuart's outnumbered troopers in a brilliant and gallant action held back Union cavalry and infantry on May 8, long enough for Confederate infantry to come to their aid and stabilize Lee's line.

The next day he learned from his outposts to the north near the old battleground of Fredericksburg that Sheridan's bluecoated troopers were heading south in great force. The length of the column which was being attacked along its line by Stuart's men was thirteen miles long

But Sheridan was riding fast.

Getting to Lee's advance supply base at Beaver Dam, north of Richmond, his troopers' rapid attack had compelled the Confederate guard forces to fire the immense amount of stores there, and then destroy whatever was left.

The long column of horse had then turned south in the direction of the Confederate capital.

Stuart had only a few minutes to kiss his wife and two children who were staying nearby farewell before turning his horsemen to the south in pursuit of the Yankee raiders.

He and his troopers got ahead of the blue raiders, so on the morning of May 11 they were able to interpose themselves between Sheridan and the capital at a place called Yellow Tavern some five or six miles north of Richmond.

Major Henry B. McClellan, Stuart's chief-of-staff, tells what happened:

"About four o'clock the enemy suddenly threw a brigade of cavalry, mounted, upon our extreme left, attacking our whole line at the same time. As he always did, the general hastened to the point where the greatest danger threatened—the point against which the enemy directed the mounted charge. . . .

"The enemy's charge captured our battery on the left of our line, and drove back almost the entire left. Where Captain Dorsey was stationed—immediately on the Telegraph Road—about eighty men had collected, and among these the general threw himself, and by his personal example held them steady while the enemy charged entirely past their position. With these men he fired into their flank and rear as they passed him, in advancing and retreating, for they were met by a mounted charge of the 1st Virginia Cavalry and driven back some distance. As they retired, one man who had been dismounted in the charge and was running out on foot turned as he passed the general and discharging his pistol inflicted the fatal wound.

"When Captain Dorsey discovered that he was wounded he came at once to his assistance, and endeavored to lead him to the rear; but the general's horse had become so restive and unmanageable that he insisted upon being taken down, and allowed to rest against a tree. When this was done, Captain Dorsey sent for another horse. While waiting, the general ordered him to leave him and return to his men and drive back the enemy. He said he feared that he was mortally wounded and could be of no more service. Captain Dorsey told him that he could not obey that order, that he would rather sacrifice his life than leave him until he had placed him out of all danger. The situation was an exposed one. Our men were sadly scattered, and there was hardly a handful of men between that little group and the advancing enemy. But the horse arrived in time; the general was lifted onto him, and was led by Captain Dorsey to a safer place. There, by the general's order, he gave him into the charge of Private Wheatly, of his company, and returned to rally his scattered men. Wheatly procured an ambulance, placed the general in it with the greatest care and, supporting him in his arms, was driven toward the rear.

"I was hastening toward that part of the field where I had heard that he was wounded when I met the ambulance. The general had so often told me that if he were wounded I must not leave the field, but report to the officer next to him in rank, that I did not now presume to disregard his order, and the more so because I saw that Dr. Fontaine, Venable, Garnett, Hullihen, and several of his couriers were attending him. I remained with General Fitz Lee until the next morning, when he sent me to the city to see General Bragg, and I thus had an opportunity to spend an hour with my general.

"As he was being driven from the field he noticed the disorganized ranks of his retreating men, and called out to them: "Go back! go back! and do your duty, as I have done mine, and our country will be safe. Go back! go back! I had rather die than be whipped."

"These were his last words on the battlefield—words not of idle egotism, but of soldierly entreaty. . . ."

That night he died.

General John Sedgwick, commander of the Union army's VI Corps, perhaps put it best when he said Jeb Stuart was "the greatest cavalry officer ever foaled in America."

Criticism of his indecision while confronting the heights of Cemetery Hill was readily acknowledged by the genial Richard Stoddert Ewell. The indecision was acknowledged but never explained.

Long after, in talking with Brigadier General Eppa Hunton, who had participated in Pickett's Charge as a colonel in Garnett's brigade, Old Bald Head cheerily admitted: "It took a dozen blunders to lose Gettysburg and he had committed a good many of them."

But no real reason was ever advanced as to why he had remained immobile in his saddle on that first day at Gettysburg while the precious golden minutes drained through the hourglass of time.

Years after, General Winfield Scott Hancock was to say: ". . . in my opinion, if the Confederates had continued the pursuit of General Howard on the afternoon of the 1st July at Gettysburg, they would have driven him over and beyond Cemetery Hill. After I arrived upon the field, assumed the command, and made my dispositions for defending that point (say 4 P.M.) I do not think the Confederate force then present could have carried it."

Confederate cannon and troops in place on Cemetery Hill would, of course, have denied Cemetery Ridge to Meade's forces and he would have had to order a withdrawal to a new position with all the risk and peril such a retrograde movement would entail.

Lee, himself, expressed his belief in later years that if Cemetery Hill could have been seized and held, the battle would have been won.

But time would move on into 1864 to find Ewell and his Second Corps sharing in the army's bitter fighting in The Wilderness and at bloody Spotsylvania.

It was after that battle that the physical condition of Ewell deteriorated so that he had to be placed on leave and eventually given command of the Richmond defenses, forcing him to take leave of his beloved troops of the Second Corps and the field duty which he gloried in.

Old Bald Head would be missed by the Army of Northern Virginia only to return to it as the shadows of Appomattox would reach out to engulf it.

Cheerful and generous, he would live out the war to retire to a farm in Tennessee.

Having spent most of his career in the Old Army in cavalry duty on the western frontier, he was renowned for his summation of his career before the war, declaring that he had learned all about commanding fifty dragoons and had forgotten everything else.

The role of the dashing Lieutenant General A. P. Hill, commanding the Third Corps, would be a puzzling, even a passive one.

It was he who had opened the battle when he sent Harry Heth's division smashing into Gettysburg "to buy some shoes," only to have them fetch up in a bloody battle with the blue troopers of John Buford on McPhersons' and later, Seminary Ridge.

Sick back in Cashtown, he would not arrive at the scene of the action until later.

When he did, he would find his Third Corps troops in a bitter battle with Federal I and XI Corps troops disputing their advance across McPhersons' Ridge.

The bluecoats had only begun to bend when Ewell's Second Corps brigades began to press down upon their line from the north.

Then the enemy had broken, retreating back into Gettysburg and up the slop   of Cemetery Hill and the Ridge which ran to the south.

Hill's soldiers pursued them to the crest of Seminary Ridge from where they watched the disorganized Federals making their way to the other side of the valley.

It was then Lee had asked Hill if his men could not go on and capture Cemetery Hill while the enemy's fighting lines were collapsing.

But it had been a savage fight to get this far.

Hill felt that his men had taken too many casualties and were too exhausted to attempt the new attack on Cemetery Hill.

He demurred.

It was this decision which forced Lee to turn to Ewell and the Second Corps.

Perhaps if Hill had not been sick it might have been different.

Perhaps.

Hill would participate with Lee and Longstreet in planning the attacks on July 2 and July 3, but it is difficult to find any imprint from him on the course of the great battle.

He, like Ewell, would fight with his Third Corps in the

thunderous battles in The Wilderness and at Spotsylvania, only to be slain by Federal riflemen before the Petersburg defenses in the closing days of the war on April 2, 1865.

When James Longstreet rode up to join Lee on Seminary Ridge about five o'clock in the afternoon of July 1, 1863, the first day of the battle, he found the commanding general busy with orders and dispatches.

While he waited, his professional soldier's eyes scanned the salient terrain features of the countryside as it lay before him.

When Lee had completed his business, he walked over to his senior lieutenant general to point out to him where on Cemetery Hill the beaten Federal troops had withdrawn in the face of the attacks delivered by Hill and Ewell that afternoon.

Old Pete then with his glasses made a careful survey of the ground fronting Seminary Ridge reaching out towards the enemy.

But he was looking at the ground from the opposite of his commanding general's point of view, for while Lee was thinking of immediate attack, Longstreet was examining the terrain with an eye to the defense of a strong position.

The two generals then began a long conference, each outlining their analysis of the battle situation.

Longstreet wanted the army to interpose itself south of the Federals they could presently see and invite Meade to attack them on ground of their own choosing.

Lee objected that this would involve great risk, that in the absence of Stuart, little or nothing was known of Meade's dispositions to the south.

He pointed out that the army had won a victory that afternoon and that victory must be exploited while the enemy units before them could be destroyed before the main force of the Army of the Potomac could come up.

Old Pete was unconvinced.

He would later write:

"Lee seemed under a subdued excitement which occasionally took possession of him when 'the hunt was up,' and threatened his superb equipoise. The sharp battle fought by Hill and Ewell on that day had given him a taste of victory."

He did not seem to realize that Lee was casting up the odds for the whole campaign: attack, defend or withdraw. Of the three Lee had chosen the attack as offering the greatest gains for the lesser risks.

He would judge: "A battle had, therefore, become in a measure unavoidable, and the success already gained gave hope of a favorable issue."

After Lee had returned from his evening conference with Ewell in the town of Gettysburg, he again met with Longstreet and Hill where he reviewed his battle plan for the coming day.

When he left the late night conference with Lee and Hill, Longstreet rode back to his own headquarters in company with his medical director Dr. J. S. Dorsey Cullen.

Upon the doctor's lauding the day's victory, Old Pete differed, saying it would have been better not to have fought at all than to leave Meade's forces holding such dominating ground.

In such a mood he retired to rise again about 3 A.M. to breakfast then ride back to Lee's observation post on Seminary Ridge. While they were talking, they were joined by Hill, then by Hood and finally McLaws.

The day was growing older when it was decided Longstreet would attack obliquely at the low point of Cemetery Ridge north of the Round Tops, then sweep up the Ridge to Cemetery Hill.

It was then that Lee had left his generals to prepare the attack, while he rode over to Ewell to coordinate the Second Corps efforts with the assault on the right.

It was only after he had returned to Seminary Ridge

sometime after eleven o'clock to find that nothing had been done that he specifically ordered Longstreet to attack with his two divisions present as soon as practicable.

Yet this was not to be so very soon. In spite of Lee's instructions, the attack, because of a fumbled approach march and the discovery of heavy formations of Sickles' III Corps well forward of Cemetery Ridge, did not get underway until about half-past three in the afternoon, this late, when Lee had been counting on an early morning assault.

When the fighting did erupt, it was ferocious. It would flare through the Round Tops, the Devils Den, the Peach Orchard, the Wheat Field, and reach right up and into the Federal cannon on Cemetery Ridge itself.

Then it would recede, the gray brigades unable to maintain the power of their assault when it had reached the objective.

As darkness ended the fighting on his line, Longstreet returned to his corps headquarters, but strangely, he did not go to Lee's headquarters or seek further orders.

For Peter Longstreet it had been a most unsatisfactory day.

Well before daylight on July 3, 1863, Lee was riding off to the right to check on Old Pete's preparations for the grand assault which was to effect a penetration of Meade's army, roll up his lines, and hopefully win the battle for the Confederacy.

While he rode along the ridge under a slightly hazy morning sky, the artillery had finished its posting of its guns, under the direction of Colonel E. P. Alexander who was determined the "Long Arm" would make a great contribution to the victory.

But when Lee came to Longstreet's field headquarters, he could see no evidence of Pickett's division which would be the core of the attack, nor any sign of a preparing offensive.

The reason?

Longstreet explained it quickly.

His scouts during the night hours had discovered that Meade's left flank beyond the Round Tops was uncovered, giving the Confederates an opportunity to move around to the south and make the Federals attack them.

Lee shook his head again, the attack on Cemetery Ridge must go in. It was the only feasible way of breaking the Union line.

When Longstreet saw that he was not going to move Lee from his purpose, he had another objection. The divisions of Hood and McLaws, which together with Pickett would make up the core of the assault column, had been so badly mauled in the second day's fighting that Longstreet recommended other units should be substituted for them.

After some discussion, Lee agreed that the new divisions would come from Hill's Third Corps. As this would delay the jump-off until 10 A.M., a courier was sent galloping to Ewell to open with his guns at that time.

But this was already too late, for Lee himself had heard the roar of artillery from Ewell's front as he had ridden to Longstreet's field headquarters.

Yet ten o'clock slipped on towards noon before the troops could complete taking their positions.

It was then the strange silence of Gettysburg enfolded the great field shimmering in the heat of a 90-degree sun.

Ewell's guns had gone silent, leaving only the distant popping of skirmishers' fire to disturb the noontide.

By his actions, Longstreet showed that he disapproved of the coming attack which would be led by his favorite George Edward Pickett.

But it could no longer be delayed.

The massed artillery, both Confederate and Union, opened on each other's lines at one o'clock in the explosive thunder of the stupendous cannonade, shocking not only men, but animals and any living thing.

Pickett and his legions had gone forward in the fiery blast of the fury of the guns. Thousands were cut down, but the assault moved on until it reached the main battle line on Cemetery Ridge, broke through it, then in a milling mass of confusion, was repelled.

Longstreet took immediate action to rally the slowly withdrawing troops and assigned his staff to the same duty.

The British Army observer Colonel Freemantle wrote in admiration:

"No person could have been more calm or self-possessed than General Longstreet under these trying circumstances, aggravated as they now were by the movements of the enemy, who began to show a strong disposition to advance. . . . Difficulties seem to make no other impression on him than to make him a little more savage."

So the preparations went forward to fend off the Federal counterattack that never came.

But the bluecoats were fought out too.

That evening as the rain swept down on the long battle lines, Lee made his way to where Longstreet sat by his bivouac campfire.

Speaking without any rancor of the afternoon's bloody repulse, Lee said:

"It's all my fault. I thought my men were invincible."

The deep personal friendship of Lee and Longstreet had emerged from the fiery maelstrom unscathed.

Long after, Longstreet would write an uncle:

"General Lee chose the plans adopted; and he is the person appointed to choose and to order. I consider it a part of my duty to express my views to the Commanding General. If he approves and adopts them, it is well; if he does not, it is my duty to adopt his views, and to execute his orders as faithfully as if they were my own. I cannot help but think that great results would have obtained had my views been thought better of; yet I am much inclined to accept the present condition as for the best. I hope and trust that it is so. . . . I fancy that no good ideas upon that campaign will be mentioned at any time, that did not receive their share of consideration of General Lee. The few things that he might have overlooked himself were, I believe, suggested by myself. As we failed, I must take my share of the responsibility. In fact, I would prefer that all the blame should rest upon me. As General Lee is our commander, he should have the support and influence we can give him. If the blame, if there is any, can be shifted from him to me, I shall help him and our cause by taking it. I desire, therefore, that all the responsibility that can be put upon me shall go there, and shall remain there. The truth will be known in time, and I shall leave that to show how much of the responsibility of Gettysburg rests on my shoulders . . ."

Longstreet would go on to fight in Tennesse before returning to Lee in the Wilderness. He would be severely wounded there and would not return to the army until it had been driven back before Petersburg.

He would be with Lee at Appomattox, where he would assist in arranging the terms of the surrender, and where he would be greeted most cordially by his old friend Grant.

He would be with Lee at the surrender.

After the war he would serve in a number of Federal government offices.

He would die in 1904.

So ran the records of Lee's chief lieutenants in the great battle.

Lee himself would take his place with the other immortals as one of the greatest soldiers of all time.

Lee was very restrained in his comments regarding the great battle, choosing instead to take all the blame for the Southern loss on his own shoulders.

A close friend, however, reported that in a conversation in 1868:

"He (Lee) found himself engaged with the Federal army . . . unexpectedly, and had to fight. This being decided on, victory would have been won if he could have gotten one decided simultaneous attack on the whole line. This he tried his utmost to effect for three days, and failed. Ewell he could not get to act with decision. Rodes, Early, Johnson attacked and were hurt in detail. Longstreet, Hill, etc. could not be gotten to act in concert. Thus the Federal troops were enabled to be opposed to each of our corps, or even divisions, in succession. As it was, however, he inflicted more damage than he received, and he broke up the Federal summer campaign."

Not long before his death, in a conversation with a close relative, he said that if Jackson had been at Gettysburg he would have held the heights that Ewell seized.

Again, while out riding with one of the professors of his college, he said:

"If I had had Stonewall Jackson with me, so far as man can see, I should have won the battle of Gettysburg."

But in the end he saved his greatest praise for those who fought, the living and the dead, at the great battle:

"The privations and hardships of the march and camp were cheerfully encountered, and borne with a fortitude unsurpassed by our ancestors in their struggle for independence, while their courage in battle entitles them to rank with the soldiers of any army and of any time."

On April 10, 1865, at Appomattox Court House where Lee had formally surrendered to General Grant the previous day, Lee was riding back to his field headquarters from a meeting with Grant who had come over to pay him a courtesy call, when he met a group of mounted Federal officers approaching him in the road.

Suddenly he was greeted with a cheery "Good morning, General," from a bearded officer who saluted him by removing his cap.

Lee did not immediately recognize the officer.

"I am George Gordon Meade," the speaker said.

The two old friends from former days and opponents at the terrible struggle at Gettysburg rode up to each other.

"What are you doing with all that gray in your beard," Lee asked.

"You have to answer for most of it!" Meade shot back.

Lee and his aides then escorted their visitors back to the Confederate field headquarters where the two commanding generals were left alone for a long talk.

It would seem that the Battle of Gettysburg was finally over.

48

Written in the Stars

THERE IS A MYSTIC QUALITY ABOUT THE BATTLE OF GETtysburg.

It holds a sense of destiny, of a foretold end.

So much of what happened there was not explained at the time, nor later. And now, never will be.

There were and are mysteries on both sides of the lines, both the Blue and the Gray.

Fate, coincidence, destiny.

Call it what you will, there were strange happenings at Gettysburg on which the future of the Great Republic and its archrival, the Confederate States of America, would hinge.

In all the many battles the United States of America would fight in the course of all its many wars, there were only two where the very fate of the nation depended upon the decision of victory or defeat.

The first of these would be Gettysburg.

The second would be Pearl Harbor.

In both of these battles, strangely enough, the final results would depend to a great degree upon the decisions and actions taken by men who were her avowed enemies.

So it was to a great extent that the future of the Republic was saved by the failure of these hostile commanders to fully utilize and exploit the openings and opportunities for inflicting devastating destruction when they held in their hands the means to do so.

Examine what happened during the Gettysburg Campaign when Lee invaded the North, and especially during those critical days of the great battle: Wednesday, Thursday, Friday, Saturday—July 1, 2, 3, and 4 in 1863.

By force of circumstances, Lee was forced to invade the North in 1863 as he had invaded in September of 1862.

In war ravaged Virginia, he was having great difficulties in feeding and supplying the Army of Northern Virginia. The prospect of doing so in the fertile valleys and farms of Maryland and Pennsylvania was a most compelling one.

An invasion of the North which would threaten the Federal capital would ensure that Union troops now in Virginia would be called north in defense of Washington at the instance of President Lincoln, thereby further lightening the burden of conflict on the South.

There was also the possibility of foreign recognition of the Confederacy and perhaps intervention by Britain and France through the means of an enforced armistice for negotiation or arbitration of the issues involved.

An invasion would also strengthen the hand of those political elements in the North which were calling for an end of the conflict and were threatening to unseat Lincoln in his campaign for reelection.

Conversely, if Lee would decide to go over to the defen-

sive with his much smaller force and much smaller re-
sources, he knew it would be only a short while before he
would be forced to stand siege before Richmond.

From then on it would only be a matter of time.

The end would be certain.

So Lee headed north.

His swift moves to send the army north caught Hooker
off guard.

The gray columns were across the Potomac and into
Maryland and up into Pennsylvania before he could react.

It was a marvelous march.

But then things would begin to go wrong.

Lee would be failed in sequence by his four major lieutenants, Generals Stuart, Hill, Ewell and Longstreet.

These failures would be devastating.

They would be made in turn by some of the most profes-
sionally outstanding soldiers on the continent.

Why?

First mystery of Gettysburg would be the disappearance
of Stuart and the pick of his troopers on June 25 not to
reappear again so far as the Army of Northern Virginia
was concerned until July 2, the second day of the great
battle. By so doing, Stuart would deprive Lee of all knowledge of the movements of the Army of the Potomac until
late in the night of June 28 when another mystery of
Gettysburg would tear the blindfold from Lee's eyes.

With Ewell far up into Pennsylvania, ready to move to
capture the state capital at Harrisburg, and Hill and Longstreet's corps still west of the mountains, the army was
loosely scattered over a wide area of Pennsylvania soil.

It was then Harrison, Longstreet's spy and scout, was
introduced into Lee's headquarters tent with a strange
story to tell: the Army of the Potomac was already north of
that river, hot on Lee's heels and it had a new commander
in General George Gordon Meade.

Once Harrison, who was an actor fond of drinking and

gambling but who nevertheless furnished Lee vital information, had left the headquarters tent, the orders flew thick and fast, recalling Ewell, bringing up Hill and Longstreet, and concentrating the army on Gettysburg.

If Harrison had not arrived at the headquarters of the army when he did, the Army of Northern Virginia might have been defeated in detail and no battle of Gettysburg would have transpired.

Next puzzle is that of A. P. Hill, who, taken sick on the eve of the battle, allowed Heth's division to blunder on towards Gettysburg without any proper screen, to be stopped first by Federal cavalry, then infantry, in bitter fighting on McPherson's and Seminary Ridges.

It was his refusal to attack Cemetery Hill on the first day which led to Ewell's failure to mount any offensive out of Gettysburg against that key Union position.

On the second and third days of the battle, the coordination of the attacks of Third Corps divisions with those of first Ewell and then Longstreet are suspect—all in all, a poor performance from the general whose division had saved the Southern right flank by its savage attack at Antietam the year before.

Then there would be Ewell.

After a brilliant start when he had devastated General Robert H. Milroy and captured the fortifications around the city of Winchester in the Shenandoah Valley, along with thousands of prisoners, to clear the way for Lee's columns to pour across the Potomac and on beyond to the unspoiled fields of Pennsylvania, his performance had been equal to that of his old commander Jackson in swift decision and rapid execution.

His march north on Harrisburg had been flawless.

And then?

When he received Lee's unsettling orders to halt the advance and retrace his steps towards Cashtown or Gettysburg, things began to come unstuck.

Even then, with his troops pouring down from the north on the beleagured Federal I and XI Corps in Gettysburg, to score another smashing victory, Old Bald Head could not make up his mind.

Urged by his own staff to seize Cemetery Hill and the key to the whole Federal position, he hesitated in the face of victory.

Instead he sought counsel which he would not accept.

When he ordered his troops forward it would be too late.

In effect he took his Second Corps out of all meaningful action after the first day at Gettysburg.

There would be no explanation forthcoming.

Nothing more would happen on Lee's left flank, where because of its exposed position Cemetery Hill might have been rendered untenable to Meade's army for the rest of the battle.

Finally there is Longstreet.

Lee's dependable war horse.

Slow and steady.

But dependable.

On these three days of all three days of the war, this would not prove to be true.

Instead Lee would be faced with interminable delays and unending argument.

Upon riding up to Lee's command post on Seminary Ridge late in the afternoon of the first day of the battle, Longstreet, after a careful examination of the enemy's position through his field glasses, proceeded without any further words to recommend to Lee defensive maneuvers which would bring on an attack by the Federal army.

Lee did not agree.

Longstreet returned to his own headquarters late that night knowing Lee intended to deliver a heavy blow on the Federal position on Cemetery Ridge as early as possible.

But when he rode up again to join Lee on the second day of the battle, he had done nothing to speed the attack which he was to deliver from the right, choosing instead to return to his arguments for a turning movement to the south to cause Meade to attack the Southern army instead.

Lee again refused him.

But Longstreet, if he could not have his way, would so delay the delivery of the attack from the right that the troops would open their assault late in the afternoon instead of early in the morning as had been planned.

Surly and obstinate, he finally sent the attack in after arguing with his division commanders and refusing to accept their scouting reports as to the enemy positions in their fore.

When these attacks were delivered with such fury that they wrecked a third Union army corps and drove into the main defense line of Meade's battle position only to recede with the coming night, the final tragic day of Gettysburg had been assured.

On this last day, Longstreet again withheld his cooperation, even his obedience, so the great attack scheduled to go in early in the morning did not advance until the afternoon.

Faced with these unexpected breakdowns in the very core of the army's command structure, is there any wonder Lee appeared nervous and somewhat distraught during the long trial of battle?

The odds for such a series of failures in the Southern high command would have been very long, indeed.

But not all mischance would be wearing gray during those heart-stopping days before, during and after Gettysburg.

At times, error and delay would don the blue.

Although Washington's spy reports, reputedly more accurate and timely than those of the South, had indicated to Hooker that Lee was preparing to move north, they were not believed or given due weight in their evaluation, until Pleasanton's cavalry dispatches compelled him to act.

By that time the Army of Northern Virginia was over the Potomac and passing through Maryland with its advance guard well into Pennsylvania.

Hooker immediately ordered his army corps to the fords of the Potomac headed for the north and Lee.

But he was late, and the North was on fire with alarm.

Hooker tried to catch up by forcing the march to interpose his army between the Confederates and the cities of Baltimore and Philadelphia while all the while covering the approaches to the City of Washington.

In making all the hurried and intricate dispositions to hurry the army northward, he lost his temper over the minor movement of troops from the Harpers Ferry garrison and sent in his resignation to General-in-Chief Henry Halleck, who advised him that the matter was out of his hands and he would have to talk to the President.

This did not take very long because Lincoln, Secretary of War Stanton, and Halleck had decided that because of Chancellorsville, Hooker would never command at another major battle.

Riding a special train with the tracks cleared for speed, a staff colonel, Halleck's emissary, roared out of the capital bound for Frederick in Maryland.

Upon his arrival there, the messenger was provided a mount to carry him to the headquarters of the V Corps where its commanding general, George Gordon Meade, was roused out of his bed at three o'clock in the morning of June 28.

At first Meade thought he was being arrested, for what he did not know.

When he learned he was to take over command of the army, he protested that there were other more qualified officers, his friend General John Reynolds being one of them.

Nevertheless, he was told, this was an order from the highest authorities and he must comply.

So the unwilling Meade had shrugged on his clothes and, along with a surprised Hooker, participated in a change-of-command ceremony in the uncomfortable hours of the early morning.

This change of commanders of the nation's chief army on the eve of a great battle was not only unprecedented but held the potential for disaster to the Army of the Potomac.

Only the good common sense of Meade held things together.

But Lincoln, Stanton and Halleck were close to the line of being derelict in their duty because of this eleventh hour transfer of command.

Once again the gods of war must have laughed.

When the battle did open, only the hours of delay gained by the tough troopers of General John Buford saved the I Corps under Abner Doubleday and the XI Corps of Otis Howard from complete disaster.

The two generals were able to salvage enough out of the wreck of their two corps to draw a line on Cemetery Hill which, if it did nothing else, intimidated Ewell enough so that he lost one of the main chances to carry the day.

On the second day of the battle, the ebullient General Daniel Sickles' stars failed to shine when he committed two major errors which almost lost the battle for the North.

First error would be his failure to obey orders to hold the Round Tops, which would be the southern anchors of Meade's long battle line. Instead, Sickles would wave these orders off in favor of shoving his III Corps far out in advance of the main defense line.

This would lead to his second great error of creating a

vulnerable salient which the Confederate infantry would assail in great force, wrecking the III Corps and imperiling the center of Meade's army along Cemetery Ridge.

Peach Orchard, the Wheat Field, and the Devil's Den would be place names forever associated with this mistake.

Meade, himself, would detract from his almost flawless performance in two regards:

First, on the third day of the battle, for some reason early in the morning he had shifted some of his troop strength northward to Cemetery Hill from the critical Cemetery Ridge line where Lee's major blow would fall.

This led to the desperate transfer of infantry along the front of Hancock's II Corps in the flaming battle for The Crest, and the final repulse of Pickett's Charge at The Little Clump of Trees.

The second mistake would be the long delay in launching the pursuit of Lee's battered army.

While it is understandable, in the shock of the terrible battle losses that the Army of the Potomac had sustained and the disarray of his own order of battle, why he could not have gone over to the offensive on the fourth day, it would be an inordinate length of time before he actively started to attempt to destroy the Army of Northern Virginia before it escaped across the Potomac.

Lincoln had said: "We had them within our grasp. We had only to stretch forth our hands and they were ours."

But it wouldn't have been that easy.

There was plenty of fight left in the Army of Northern Virginia.

Perhaps the key player in the drama of Gettysburg was Death, himself.

Besides holding high carnival over the carnage of the great battle field, he had called to him two soldiers who, if they had lived, might have exerted the influence on the flow of the battle which could have turned it this way or that.

First would be that great soldier, that commander, that executive officer without peer—Thomas Jonathan Jackson.

In all the episodes of the battle from the Southern point of view, his absence is most crucial.

Dynamic in his conception of battle, swift and forceful in his execution of plans and orders, his absence would leave a void which would go unfilled.

This absence was perhaps best explained by a remark of one of Ewell's staff officers who had served under the great commander.

Waiting for Old Bald Head to issue orders to the Second Corps to attack and capture Cemetery Hill on the first day of the battle, this officer, watching Ewell in the town square of Gettysburg, turned to another fellow officer to say: "Jackson is not here."

Second key death would be that of General John Reynolds, commander of the Union's I Corps, who was shot from his horse as he was urging troops forward to reinforce Buford's cavalry line opposing Heth's attack on McPherson's Ridge on the first day of battle.

Meade, himself, felt that command of the Army of the Potomac should have gone to Reynolds.

Reynolds was recognized throughout the army as one of the paramount soldiers of the North.

His death would leave two adequate but not brilliant commanders in Doubleday and Howard to try to stem the Confederate tide as it swept onwards toward Cemetery Hill.

Their troops would finally hold. But it would be a ragged effort.

If Ewell had attacked with vigor, there would have been a question.

A very great question indeed.

So in the end, the decision to be rendered at Gettysburg would depend in great degree on the state of mind of four of the key players on the Southern side.

Opposed to this would be the devoted and coolly professional direction of the battle by the general officers gathered about that stubborn fighter, George Gordon Meade.

For the performance of the soldiers and officers of both the North and the South, there would be little to choose.

It would be superb.

Still, the unsettling question of Gettysburg is the same as that posed by the attack on Pearl Harbor.

If the attacking commanders had had a different mind-set, what would have been the outcome of the battle and the war?

The great Russian, Leo Tolstoy, believed that the course of events shapes the major flow of history, with the actions of men and women not counting for all that much:

". . . all the innumerable individuals who took part in the war (the invasion of Russia by Napoleon in 1812) acted in accordance with their natural dispositions, habits, circumstances and aims. They were moved by fear or vanity, they rejoiced or were indignant, they argued and supposed that they knew what they were doing and did it of their own free will, whereas they were all the involuntary tools of history, working out a process concealed from them but intelligible to us. Such is the inevitable lot of men of action, and the higher they stand in the social hierarchy the less free they are."

Admiral Chester Nimitz held a different view.

Confronted with the same possibilities of absolute disaster facing the United States at Gettysburg, some 78 years later at Pearl Harbor and then Midway, Nimitz against almost hopeless odds resolutely brought victory out of the chaos of defeat.

After that titanic struggle, he was later to write:

"Just why the Japanese navy failed to complete the havoc and destruction at Pearl Harbor, which was easily in their power, must be left to another story.

"But the attack shocked our country out of its apathy about the world war already under way in Europe. All the arguments for and against entering the conflict ended and America, as one man, joined the fight against aggression.

"Can anyone doubt that, during those momentous years of World War II, an all-seeing Divine Providence was guiding and protecting our nation as, indeed, it had from the days of our Revolution?"

In the end, that sturdy soldier George Gordon Meade may have said it all.

Riding up the crest of Cemetery Hill to look out over the vast field covered by the retreating thousands of Pickett's Charge, he took off his hat to give a cheer for victory.

But it wouldn't come.

Solemnly bringing his hat down to his side, he simply said: "Thank God!"

Key Commanders at Gettysburg

Army of Northern Virginia

	General Robert E. Lee, Commanding
First Corps:	Lieutenant General James Longstreet
Second Corps:	Lieutenant General Richard Stoddert Ewell
Third Corps:	Lieutenant General Ambrose Powell Hill
Cavalry Corps:	Major General James Ewell Brown Stuart
Artillery:	Colonel E. Porter Alexander

Army of the Potomac

	Major General George Gordon Meade, Commanding
I Corps:	Major General John Reynolds/Major General Abner Doubleday
II Corps:	Major General Winfield Scott Hancock/Major General John Gibbon
III Corps:	Major General Daniel Sickles/Major General John Newton
V Corps:	Major General George Sykes
VI Corps:	Major General John Sedgwick
XI Corps:	Major General Oliver Otis Howard
XII Corps:	Major General Henry Slocum
Cavalry Corps:	Major General Alfred Pleasanton
Artillery:	Major General Henry J. Hunt

Federal Corps was about half the size of the Confederate Corps.